# *THE NAKED FLAME*

*A Novel*
*by*
*Mick Donnellan*

MICK DONNELLAN

Mick Donnellan is the author of three previous novels. El Niño (2012) Fisherman's Blues (2014) and Mokusatsu (2019). When not writing fiction he works as a successful Playwright and Screenwriter. Film credits include Tiger Raid (2016) adapted from Mick's Play Radio Luxembourg. You can read more on
*www.mickdonnellan.com*

*For lovers everywhere.*

MICK DONNELLAN

## Loose Blue Dress

Behold the stirred machinery of the soul. Here she is, our first guest, a hooker on a Sunday afternoon. Her name is Marilyn. Wearing a loose blue dress and red high heels. Brown eyes and long washed black hair.

We were in Madrid, Spain. *Casa de Campo.* Sunshine, the hum of siestas, hangover. She smiled, asked: 'Lost?'

Surprised at her English, I said: 'I thought you'd speak Spanish.'

'Do you want me to speak Spanish?'

I shrugged and she asked: 'Do you have a car?'

'No. I'm here on my stag night.'

'I don't care. Do you want something or not?'

After our crime, behind some trees and a billboard, she said: 'You haven't done this before.'

'Does that bother you?'

'Only thing that bothers me is money.'

'How much?'

'Let's call it €40.'

I stepped back, stood on a bag of rubbish and fell over. Smell of rotten food. She put her hands to her mouth and giggled. I stood up, embarrassed. Searched my pockets. Found my wallet. Handed her the cash. Shewas back to business, took it and put it somewhere.

I said: 'So, that's it?'

'You'll be here again. If not with me, with someone else.'

'How do you mean?'

'You're one of the guilty ones.'

'I don't understand.'

'Are you going to tell your girl?'

'I don't know.'

'That means *no*.'

'Why do you care?'

'Who said I cared? You're scaring away business. Now piss off.'

I turned to walk, head spinning like a gyroscope. Then I turned back and asked: 'Where did you learn such good English?'

'I was born in London.'

'Can I buy you a drink?'

'No.'

'Lunch?'

She looked me up and down. 'Treating me well isn't going to take back what you did.'

'I don't want to take it back.'

'You need sleep.'

'I want to know you.'

'You're delirious.'

'Probably.'

She lit a cigarette, said: 'I'm here til six.'

'I'll see you then. My name is John joe...'

'Bye *John joe*.'

Somewhere, a car beeped. We both looked over. Black BMW. A man inside. Tattoos, earrings, muscles. Pure telly pimp. Two years from now he'll be dead. Gangland shooting. Ricochet bullet. Today, he's very much alive. He tapped his wrist. She sighed and said: 'You better go.'

Found Gran Via, the main boulevard of Madrid. Commercial

applause, or shiny bright steel reality, haunted by majestic statues. Discovered a Starbucks. Drank fancy coffee. Six o'clock came. Crepuscular sundown, punctuated by loud traffic and city drenched possibility.

I went back. Plasma acupuncture. She walked over, said: 'I'm surprised.'

I handed her a Mocha, went: 'You're probably tired.'

'It's been a busy day. I'm starting to think you have mental problems. Did you call your girl?'

'No.'

'I knew you were a coward.'

'Let's get a real drink.'

We found a bright pub with a steel counter and two empty stools. The evening came, dark, cold; and full of possibility. I got drinks, vodkas, just to set things in motion. She drank it like a milkshake, said: 'So, where you from?'

'Athlone.'

'Is that a country?'

'It's a place in Ireland. Here for the weekend for the stag.'

'You enjoy it?'

'*You're* kind of the highlight so far.'

'Great. I've never done this for *free* before.'

'Oh. Are we…?'

'I'm not charging. It's nice to be treated human for a while.'

'I'm confused. You're gorgeous, seem educated and…'

'And I'm not even real.'

'Not a real hooker?'

'I'm just a fantasy.'

'A fantasy?'

'I'm a figment. Some childhood film clip you're playing

from your head. You find me sexy?'

'I find you sexy.'

'You meet a hooker in a park and bring her for a drink. What're you trying to play out?'

'I don't know.'

'You don't know. Behold the stirred machinery of the soul.'

'That's what I thought when I saw you.'

'I see into you. I know men. You're a dreamer, and a lover, and you're running from something. Running into my arms like I have all the answers. Like a Greek warrior looking for the magical mist of a Goddess to show him the way back from the horrors of war.'

'And can you?'

'Can I save you?'

'Can you save me?'

'Everybody wants to be saved all the time. What's the point? Is it such a terrible affliction to be alive? Just let go and be in Hell and get it over with. All this pining for purity and salvation and the cure for guilt. Why bother?'

'You think you're in Hell?'

'I think I'm aware. I like what I do. I'm fucking good at it and I don't apologise to the gestapo moralismo....and guess what? The Hell we're all afraid of is fucking beautiful.'

'Fuckin beautiful.'

'Fuck-*ing* beautiful. Why now?'

'Why what?'

'The week before your wedding.'

'It's complicated.'

'Do you love her?'

'Not really. And we're not sleeping together.'

'Why not?'

'She wants to wait til we're married.'

She laughed, said: 'What are you? Some kind of repressed Irish virgins?'

'No. We've slept together before. But now she thinks we were punished because of it.'

'Punished how?'

'It's a long painful story.'

'Don't bother then.'

'I won't. Do you want another drink?'

'Of course I do. I want to get drunk and then I want you to fuck me properly.'

'I didn't do it right the first time?'

'You were hopeless.'

More vodkas with coke. The shots were large and we split one mixer.

David Bowie through the speakers with *Velvet Goldmine.* It synced well with the scene, brought her face into focus. Deep unblemished skin, smooth and brown, and flawless. Mercurial eyes and layered black hair. Thin arms, thin legs, impossibly thin. And a scent like a door to a place you've been looking for.

On went the night, a trip in the excited dark, desire illuminated. I said: 'We better be careful; we could fall in love.'

'Or I could spike your drink and steal your kidneys.'

'That's not part of my fantasy at all.'

'Then drink up and let's go.'

In the hotel, she got naked and went to the shower.

I ordered room service, put the phone down and listened to the water run. I gave it a minute, then followed.

There. We transcended time and death and fear and stole a slice of peace from the cruel blizzard of ugly life. After, the food was here. Steel pots over the plates. Just like the films. I poured some Tiger beer and took in her sweet scent as she sat on the bed.

Sleek wet hair. Them arms.

There was a load of missed calls on my phone. 'The rest of the lads are lookin for me.'

'Turn it off. You're with a prostitute. Isn't that what stag nights are all about?'

In the morning. We went again. It was different sober. More intimate, real, sensory. Biting, bruising, rough but tender. Generous greed, dominant erogeny and full exhaustion of everything we had. We both came, beautifully came, supernova lovemaking, like mutual fusion among the oceans of cum and pleasure.

Calm aftermath, like two satisfied stars in the serene wilderness of space.

Warm sheets, somehow luscious. We felt the trapeze artist swing, suspended in the Spanish noise, holding back the future until he caught the next rope. Until then. We were. All things and nothing. We were. Immortal.

Then. She took a deep breath, caressed my face. I felt like I'd known her for years. She said: 'I have to go to work.'

It sounded so normal, she might have been a waitress. I moved closer, said: 'Stay.'

'You have a flight home.'

'I don't want this to end.'

'Everything has to end. It was just a fantasy, remember?'

'I'll stay.'

'You won't. This is as good as it's ever going to be. Aren't you worried I'll do the same thing tonight? With somebody else?'

'Will you?'

She didn't answer. A flash of sadness over her face. Some memory, some intrusive pain. She got out of the bed, tied up her hair and went to the bathroom. I looked at the ceiling for a while, wondering. Then she came back and pulled on her dress and said: 'You can walk me to the door. After that, we go our separate ways.'

'Do you not feel anythin at all?'

'What do you think?'

We walked down the stairs, toward the front door, suffered disapproving looks from the staff. She didn't seem to care. Outside, the day was busy and the light hurt our eyes. The streets were crowded, the traffic jammed, our time together held under a guillotine. I said: 'So this it?'

'Aren't you relieved?'

'No, just scared.'

She gave it a second, then kissed me and walked away.

After she left, I was sick with drink and loneliness. Felt dizzy and volatile. Clammy and anxious. I went back through the cool floor and upstairs to pack. In the room, her scent was still in the air, like a plane I'd missed to a better place. Her shape in the covers of the bed, on the pillow, her towel on the ground. Her brown legs haunted me. How light she was. The shimmer of her blue dress, an oceanic glimmer, a sea of something more, cut short by time and circumstance.

I brushed my teeth and thought about Ireland. Something burned and growled in my stomach, like a car in the wrong gear. I turned off the tap and everything went quiet. My reflection looked different, like a stranger. Bloodshot eyes and age torn skin. The cleaners hovered around outside, muttering Spanish questions.

Later, in a nearby pub, I drowned a fast wine. It tasted good, like twenty more. I'd already missed the flight. Not sure if I was relieved or worried. Time to chance reality. Turned on the phone.

27 missed calls.

17 voicemails.

37 SMS.

I turned it off and ordered another drink. Wedding in a week and me here in Madrid riding hookers. Great job, John joe.

I got nicely pissed. Hoping for sedation. Numbness. Answers.

Ate some Tapas. The omelettes were alright but I wouldn't chance the olives. I took a look around. Fat Spaniards mostly. Small stools. Soccer on the telly. A smell like vinegar. Life was good here, laid back, calm. Same as everywhere when you're on holidays. I thought about going back to find Marilyn. Then said I better not. I had the fear, the horrors, I wasn't right. So I had five or six more wines and left to face the guilty music.

Rang Karen on the way to the airport. That was her. The one I was marrying.

She went mental. Where the fuck was I? Did I not know there was uncles flying in from America on Tuesday? A problem with the flowers. One of the band had had a heart attack and the limo driver's car was after failing the NCT and what the fuck now?

I hung up and took the next flight going. It cost a bomb and took four hours.

Then I was in Dublin. Came through the arrivals. Nothing to declare.

A smell like exhaust and tar when I left the terminal.

Found the car. Opel Vectra. Metallic blue.

Fifteen years old and she still drove like new.

Fucked the bags in the back and sat in. The steering wheel was firm and ready for action. I turned the ignition, let the glow plugs warm, then fired her up.

It started with a purr. The radio blasted in with Lyric FM. *Tchaikovsky*. It always opened on that station somehow. Every time you started the car you got a blast of classical. I switched it to Tom Dunne's *Pet Sounds*. He was banging out some Bowie -

*Under Pressure.* Figure that.

Was I alright to drive? Highly unlikely. Had the guts of a barrel of wine drank in Madrid and a few whiskys on the plane. But I had to get home.

It was this or the *Citylink*.

And fuck the *Citylink*.

## *Sweet Jehovah*

Out we went. On to the M50. Took the M4 at Liffey Valley and merged on to the M6 at Kinnegad. Kept her steady. Wasn't too bad when I had one eye closed and the music going loud and the window open. Was wondering how I'd feel when I'd see Karen. You know that first second? The guilt. Was it the only time I'd cheated? Not really. But still. You know yourself? She didn't deserve it. She had that Irish devotion thing going on. Wouldn't dream of cheating herself. And sure that only made it worse. Then again, there was fuck all fireworks in the bedroom lately. Fuck all for the last year. And by *fuck all* I mean *fuckin nothing*. How's that work, your honour? Mind the wall there, John joe. Fuck sake.

Had I drink at the house? I did. A few cans and that gammy bottle of wine from the hamper Karen had won at work. Sweet Jehovah. I could almost taste it. Sank the shoe and drove on.

Eventually arrived in Athlone.

Got off at the Birr exit and went in through town. The weather was dark and cold, like a childhood illness. Traffic slow and calm. January weather, like an orange lozenge of dying winter's hope. Went over the bridge with the Shannon on the left. The river breathes, glimmers, silent ripples and small waves. Wind blows like crystallised pain. Came around by the Left Bank. Men at pub doors singing the cancer angelus, smoking the dead smoke. Rain falls now, unrelenting, like it has something to prove. Life beats like a dance tune, rolling wheels of the car, dark melting buildings through the drop drenched windscreen.

Tom Dunne banging out Pearl Jam. The first echoes of *Alive.* Street wet puddles. Refracted amber light, the scent of infinity, snapchild electric; let the chorus of angels sing. Almost sober by now. The irony. Got to the apartment on Connaught Street. Underground carpark. Drove in and killed the engine and let the silence settle. Settling silence. Turned off the radio. Listened to the whispering breeze above and the stillness of the cars all around and the motorized zeitgeist of dead combustion.

My mouth was dry. Parched. I got out. Picked up the bags. I used the fob to lock the car and it made a loud squawk, like it was after getting electronically kicked. Up the stairs. Got to the door. Twisted the key and walked in with a dizzy swoosh, like when you're on a skyscraper and can see through the floor. Everything at the apartment looked rearranged, cloned, unfamiliar, unreachable, trapped behind bulletproof glass. Everything I touched felt borrowed and undeserved. Karen was busy. Coming and going. She was in good shape for the wedding. Blue jeans. Blonde hair. Huge tits. Terribly organised. I wanted to hold her and feel ok but I didn't feel entitled. All she asked was: 'How did it go?'

'Grand now.'

'Anythin I should know?'

'Not a thing.'

'Good.'

She even had the dinner made. Two chops and three spuds and a few carrots. There was a list of things on the table to be done tomorrow. Picking up suits. Sorting out shoes. Something to do with rings. Hotels. Corkage. That fuckin Limo.

Then she left. Drinks somewhere. Some college friends around. Shite talk.

I went back to the room. It was cold and felt new, but somehow safe.

Left the bag down and lay on the bed and looked at the ceiling. For a second I felt like crying. It caught me like a wave, unprepared, unarmed, unexpected. A storm of emotion threatened to explode. Behind it was some kind of resolution, some unthinkable answer. I thought of Marilyn. The wealth of happiness and freedom and the Spanish air. Theft, a stolen purchase of passion.

My stomach still burned. Told myself it was the drink. The fear. The nerves. I'd be alright after a few days. I got up and went back to the kitchen and found that hamper. It was full of chocolates, cheese, and two bottles of *Faustino*.

Opened the wine.

Slaughtered it.

A few days later. I didn't feel any better. Sleeping bad, thinking mad. The fear of the altar, the shining rings, the betrayal in the vows, like drinking a world of poisonous lies.

Then. We were sitting down. Having a cup of tea. Karen was going through the guestlist on the laptop. Making sure the seating plans were ok. She was in her pyjamas. Her hair in a pure tight bun. The light of the screen twinkling off her blue eyes.

It was awful quiet besides. Like my grandparent's house when I was a child and it was late and time to say the rosary. I was eating a Yorkie now, thinking about having a wank later. Hoping it might help me sleep. I still had an awful dose of the heebie jeebies. Fairly sure I was hearing them voices last night too. *Are you there, John Joe? We need to talk to you.* Fuck me.

Then Karen pushed down the screen with a clap and asked if Jack had the Best Man Speech ready. The computer gulped and died. Like it knew this was a controversial topic. Jack was a pure header. Karen loved Jack. The same way as she loved disorganized people.

Which meant not at all.

Worse still, I hadn't even talked to him since before the stag. As far as I knew he wasn't even coming to the wedding, never mind be the Best Man. So I took a casual sip of tea and said: 'He's a 100%.'

'And there's no bad language in it?'

'Don't think so.'

'I wouldn't trust him for a second.'

'He'll come through.'

'Does he know I want him to stay sober until after the meal?'

'I'll let him know.'

'What? You haven't told him?!'

'Not yet, no.'

'I don't want him puking into my father's beef. And another thing...I heard he was at a wedding last year and he tried to steal the wedding cards and the police had to come and get him at five o'clock in the morning.'

'Yeah, but...'

'But what John joe?! Seriously! But what?'

Then my phone rang.

'Who's that?' Asked Karen.

I looked at it, said: 'Some foreign number.'

'It looks like it's from England?'

'Probably a scam.'

'Answer it.'

'Why?'

'It could be a relation stuck in Heathrow or something.'

'Ringin *me*?'

'Who knows?'

'Fuck it, be grand.'

I was about to hit *reject* when she tried to grab it.

'Ok, hang on! I'll answer.'

Silence first. Karen's head beside me listening. Her hair tickling my nose. She shouted in: 'Is that you, Eddie?!'

I'm like: *Who the fuck is Eddie?* But anyway.

A man's Spanish voice stuttered.

'Hola...?'

I said: 'Hello?'

'Is that yon yo....?'

'Heh?'

'Mr. Athlone Hon Yo...?

'Sorry.'

'Who are you looking for?' Shouted Karen.

He put in real effort the third time and asked all slow: 'Mr...John...Joe? From Ata...loan...'

'Who wants to know?'

That's when Karen saw the look on my face. The one that had flashbacks of Marilyn. She asked: 'Who the hell is it?!'

'Lady from Spain wannss to speak wit youuu....' Said the voice.

Karen very concerned now, the truth coming together, making the speed of light look slow. She asked: 'What *lady from Spain*?'

I hung up. Said: 'How do I know?'

'You know well!'

'Sure it's a scam.'

'They know your name. That you're from Athlone.'

'Shtill. Nothin to do with me.'

'Did you meet her at your stag? In Madrid? Is *that it*?'

'No.'

Her voice went up a few decibels, started to sound like feedback through a bad amplifier. 'Tell the truth, John joe. We're getting married in a week for God's sake!'

'That *is* the truth.'

'She's a hooker, isn't she?'

'No.'

'No? Really. You expect me to believe that?'

Silence, the earth breaks somewhere. Impregnable rocks crumble. Then I said: 'Ok, I did meet a hooker.'

'A what?'
'I know.'
'You slept with a *hooker*?'
'I didn't pay her the second time.'
'Are you serious?'
'Yeah. She didn't charge.'
'What the hell is wrong with you?!'
'I was scared. Cold feet. I don't know...'
'You get cold feet so you sleep with a prostitute?'
'It's what stags are all about. Marilyn said so too.'
'Who THE HELL is Marilyn?'

'That's *her.* That's her name. And it's not like me and you are up to much in that department...'

Her face went apoplectic. Pure purple rage. Then she said: 'Oh my FUCKING God!'

And she knocked me unconscious. Think she used the laptop.

Woke up and all my stuff was packed and she was gone somewhere.

Then the phone rang again.

I answered and the same voice asked: 'Cun you speek now Mr. *Yon* Joe?'

'I can. What's wrong?'

'You will come to London....'

'Is that a question?'

'When you come to be here, Mr. Ataloan...?'

'I'll have to look up flights. Be nice to know what you want too?'

'See you tomorrow. Marilyn will make waiting....'

'Why London? What happened Madrid? Is Marilyn alright?'

'Please no police....'

'Ileh?'

'Please, no police talk to you.'

'Police?'

'Yes. Please no. They come for you. We don't want.'
And he hung up. The weird bollox.

Oceanic glimmer. Blue dress. London. How're ya fixed?

## Carmina Burana

The laptop was still on the table. Thank fuck it still worked. I tore open the Ryanair site and found a fast flight.

€50.

One way.

Give it to me.

Anywhere but here.

I got to the part where they were looking for money. I was skint after Madrid. Looked around, hoped for the best. Spotted Karen's credit card beside the kettle. Deadly. Probably left there after paying for some wedding shite.

Used that.

After, I got up and went to the jacks. Fast piss. Then picked up the Karen bags and threw them in the car.

Off again. Great life.

Downstairs, grey underground parking. A graveyard of dead waiting cars. Vectra like a loyal horse, ready for road. Sat in, let the atoms assemble, figure out who was here. Turned the ignition, big blast of *Carmina Burana: O Fortuna* from *Lyric FM*. It filled the car. Suited the chaos well. Damien Omen job. Put her in first and drove up the ramp and appeared on Connaught Street like a chariot from hell. The bubbles of reality wobbled while I decided which way to go. I was in serious need of a pint, to settle the nerves and think. The Russian choir cruised my blood as I revved the engine in wired impatience.

Quare looks from pedestrians. Decided to hit *The Shack*. Dark parking. Should be quiet. Took the right after Golden Island and there it was, like an oasis in the manic Sahara. Parked up. Couple of extras smoking at the door as I walked in. Pristine counter. Cosy lights. Open fire. Few lads working on a trad session up the back. I felt safe. Relieved. Dedicated. Sure.

The news was on. It was all bad. Sat at the bar. Beermats. Drip trays. All that.

Paddy was working. Obese. Stubble. Wheezy. Apnoea. Three years he'll be dead. Sudden Adult Death Syndrome. Tonight, he's very much alive. He wanted my order. I went for a Cider. Threw it back like a confident dream. Let the glass hit the counter. The bubbles mount. Blood stream ethanol, synaptic frazzles.

He filled another pint and said: 'I heard the weddin's off.'

'Tis. Was Karen in?'

'No. She told my missus. You got caught offside?'

'Happens when the hooker's friends ring the house…'

'What they want?'

'To meet me in London.'

'Was the stag not in Madrid?'

'Twas.'

'Strange.'

'Tis.'

'Are you in trouble with the guards by any chance?'

'No, why?'

'Cos they're outside.'

And they were. Flashing lights. Yellow jackets. Curious looks around, like they'd never seen a pub door before. This made me nervous, guards always do. That's when I heard the telly mention Athlone. I looked up and they had a picture of Marilyn. I got excited, like I could wave and she might wave back.

Paddy asked: 'They say somethin about Athlone?'

'That's her.'

'Who?'

'The hooker from Madrid. Fuck it you just missed her.'

'Why the fuck's she on the telly?'

'I don't know.' I said. 'Maybe she won the lotto.'

'Maybe she's dead. Did you kill her? You sick bastard.'

'What the fuck would I be doin sittin here if I *killed* her?'

'Well someone's after gettin killed according to this.'

The door opened. The first guard entered. Grey hair. Shiny black shoes. Gave it a second to stand with his hands in his pockets. Assess the situation. Then the other one walked in. He was younger, more agile, empowered. They both approached the counter.

The older one took the lead with: 'How's Paddy?'

'Lads.'

'John joe?'

I took a drink, said: 'Howye.'

They kept focused on me. 'Were you away over in Spain last weekend?'

'I was.'

'Anythin unusual happen?'

'I met a nice lady called Marilyn.'

'Anythin else?'

'No, not that I can remember.'

'I think you better come with us for a chat.'

'Why?'

'There's people lookin for you.'

'Who's that?'

'You'll know soon enough. Did you do anythin on her?'

'Marilyn? Like what? *Hurt* her?'

'Yeah, or…. anythin weird?'

Paddy asked: 'Like tie her up? Or date rape her? Or somethin…?'

Everyone let that settle. Then I said: 'No. It was sort of intimate.'

'Aren't they all? Do we need the handcuffs or will you leave with us quietly?'

'Can I finish my pint first?'

'Do.'

'Will ye have one?'

'No thanks.'

'Ok, I'll go to the jacks. Back in a minute.'

'Don't be long. These other crowd have no patience at all.'

'What other crowd?'

'They're on the way.'

'Jesus. What's it all about?'

'We'll know in the next hour or two. Go on, have a piss and we'll go.'

In the toilet. Urinals. Smell like bleach. Big window. I fitted out through it handy enough. Fell on to the back alley and into a puddle of dirty water. Cut my hand, hurt my elbow. Saw stars for a second. Almost puked the cider. Stood up and looked around. Saw the Vectra and ran over.

Got there. Sat in. The interior sighed, like it was saying: *What now?*

I turned the key and there was a blare of haunting salsa music, South American beat. I got an image of that big crucifix in Brazil, and sun drenched madness, and my blood burnt dry from drink, like steam rising from liquid copper. Anyway, I put it in gear, and faced for the airport.

Messy.

## Diamond Rocks

Things were getting interesting. No doubt about it. I was cruising up the M6. The car strong, like a passenger jet. Tearing up the night. Kept an eye on the mirrors for the big blue lights but no sign. Then the phone rang. I looked at the screen. Unfamiliar number. Who the fuck is this now? Madrid lunatics? Irish guards? Fuck only knows.

I answered and heard: 'Hello…Karen?'

'No, do I sound like Karen? This is John joe.'

'Oh, John joe? Hi…this is Fidelma.…'

It meant nothing until she said: 'The *photographer*? For your *wedding*?'

'Oh right, yeah, Fidelma, howya.…'

'Hi, just calling to double check. Am…I heard a rumour, so I don't know…is it still going ahead or…?'

'Is what goin ahead? The weddin?'

'Yeah, I saw something online and…'

'Yeah, I think we might postpone it for a while, Fidelma…'

This seemed to be the note she didn't want to hear because she answered with: 'Oh right.'

'I know.'

'See I've turned down other bookings now cos I thought it was going ahead…'

'Sure I thought it was goin ahead too…'

'I know, but you see, it means I'm out of pocket…'

She raised her voice when she said *pocket*. Just for emphasis. Then she asked: 'Do you understand?'

'I don't think so.'

'Well, I'll need to get paid.'

'For what?'

'The wedding.'

'The one that's not goin ahead?'

'Yeah. You booked me. So….'

'So…?'

'So, what are you goin to do about it?'

'Fuck all I'd say, Fidelma.'

'That's not very nice.'

'Well I'm not goin to pay you for doin nothin…'

'Well, see, Karen said at the time that she would pay a fee upfront, and then we kind of forgot about it because she seemed so sure, I didn't push it, but now she's not answering her phone and….'

This was like something that might make me crash the car so I said: 'Ok, I can transfer you some money.'

'Really?'

'Yeah, how much was it?'

'€800 upfront deposit and then another €1200 on the day.'

'You must be good.'

Relieved laugh, then. 'Yeah. I stay busy.'

'Ok, can you text me your details and I'll send you over that deposit straight away. Will that do?'

'Ok, I'll do that now. That's perfect. Thanks, John joe.'

'No problem. €800, is it?'

'Yeah, please.'

'Sound.'

'Ok, bye.'

And she hung up. The little bitch. Five seconds later a message arrived with her bank details and a smiley face at the end. I deleted it straight away and fucked the phone out the window.

Drove on satisfied. Then thought: 'Shite! I'll need that in London!'

So I had to reverse back and spend the next ten minutes looking for it in an ugly ditch. I found it when it started ringing. Beside a dirty puddle and wet stones and ignorant weeds. It lit up the dark with chronic sound and light. I picked it up, put the mucky receiver to my ear, felt the cold go through me. Sheath like razor blades of wind. No hope against it. Just let it cut you up.

'Hello, John joe?'

'Yeah.'

'This is Christy Casey here from *Diamond Rocks*...'

'Who?'

'The band ye booked for the weddin...did someone say ye're changin the venue to Madrid instead or...?'

'Ah for fuck's sake.'

And I hung up.

## *Mam*

Airport again. The excitement of escape. Erotic thoughts of Marilyn. And that silent roar of her silk dress sliding above her hips. Her nipples in my mouth, her tongue around my scrotum, the taste of her passion sweet on her neck, like tangerines made from the mist of sexual glory.

Parked in the same carpark.

Different spot. Walked towards the terminal. Through the oncoming human traffic. Through the years of lives gone by, souls like faded canned laughter, unseen but loudly there and gone forever. The bridge of dead beginnings, a melted warp of stranger's faces, like a photograph too close to a flame. I could feel it my hands, manifested needles of electricity, and I was wired, and ready, and deaf with the crash of things collapsing.

Now. Here's a taxi rank. Gammy guards in their high viz gear.

Buses. People smoking, waiting. Crying goodbye. Hugging hello. Night time aura above. The rumble of planes, the roar of the sky economy.

Walked through the sliding doors. Doors sliding. Smell of burnt coffee and wet luggage and cosmetics. Televisions listing a myriad of countries. Scanned the departures for London. Found it. Sound. Made my way over.

Not too sure where Karen's brother came from. One minute I was bursting for a piss, looking around for a toilet, next thing he was there. Diminutive. Bushy hair. Monkish rural style of the generation unrode. Hangover from the old days when riding for pleasure was a sin.

His name was Conal. I was expecting a slap. A bollocking. Where the fuck are *you* goin? That kinda thing. Instead he smiled and said: 'John joe, how's things? All set for the wedding?'

He hadn't a clue, so I went: 'Yeah, can't wait.'

'Where you off ta?'

Thought fast with: 'I've a sick cousin in London.'

'Oh, jeez, sorry to hear that. Is it bad?'

'Fairly. Where you goin yourself?'

My bowel flipped with suspense until he said: 'London, too!'

'Oh, right. Were you talkin to Karen?'

'No, my phone's dead. I haven't heard from anyone in hours. Prefer it that way. More time to think and contemplate the real world.'

'How's that goin for you?'

'Mighty now. I feel cleansed.'

'Cleansed?'

'Like there's more to life than *social media...*'

'There is. Sure you might as well throw the phone in the bin altogether.'

'Hahah.'

The I asked: 'What's bringing *you* to London?'

'Job interview.'

'What's the job?'

'Primary school teacher.'

'Lovely.'

Christ. The silence hit. I was wondering how I'd get rid of him. Was fairly locked in. There was only one escape.

I said: 'Will you have a pint?'

'Oh, I don't drink. I'll have a coke with you, though.'

'A coke? Right, sure. The bar's up here.'

Had a piss first. Almost burst the urinal with the pressure.

Upstairs. The bar was long and white. Peppered with foreigners and too much emphasis on coffee. Still, I felt home. The pint came in a tall narrow glass nearly the height of myself. Conal wasn't used to pubs, had the look of a man that should have joined the priesthood. Then I remembered there was something about Maynooth before. He glanced around the place, looking at everyone, like it was an art exhibition. That woman in the red dress. Her legs had him staring for a good ten seconds. She caught him looking and he got all embarrassed and nervous and looked way. Then he turned to me, went: 'What's the final count for the wedding?'

*Oh yeah, that.*

'400.'

'Wow!'

'There's about 25 people I know and 375 I've never even heard of.'

'Me and Eimear are thinking of getting engaged too but we didn't want to steal Karen's thunder so we're waiting until after.'

Thunder. I got an image of Eimear. It wasn't good. Had to order a double Brandy to get over it. Conal took another sip of the useless coke and said: 'It's weird. I never really got to know you, even though you've been around our family for years.'

'Sure you were gone a lot.'

'And you were drunk a lot.'

'I was, thank fuck.'

'Sorry?'

'Nothin.'

'I never thought Karen would end up with someone like *you* if I'm honest.'

'Is that right?'

'No offence.'

'Who'd you think she'd end up with?'

'I don't know. Someone with a proper job maybe....'

'Like your dad? An auctioneer?'

'Exactly.'

'Weren't you goin to be a priest?'

'I was. But I lost my calling.'

'Why?'

'I don't think it was there to begin with. Just Mam wanted me to do it. I still read the bible though.'

Mam.

'And besides.' He continued. 'I've more of a passion for the kids than I do for the religion.'

'I wouldn't advertise that too loud, Conal.'

He looked for the insinuation. Then it hit him like a tidal wave of shame. 'What? Oh! No!! I didn't mean I...I was talking about teaching...not...'

'It's ok, I know what you mean.'

'But...'

'It's ok. Relax. I know what you were tryin to say. I've to make a phone call. Will you be alright here for a second?'

'Ye...yeah.' He stuttered. And took another wallop of coke, the ice rattling in the terrified glass. I threw back the Brandy and walked downstairs, looking around, like I was James Bond and the cameras were rolling fast, soaking up my bulletproof style.

Then I rang the guards.

999.

When I got through I said: 'My name is Conal McGuire and I'm in the airport bar with a bomb.... I blame the church.'

And I hung up.

Mam is going to love this.

## Buckled up

Conal got arrested. There was a bit of commotion first. Like when they found him and tackled him to the ground. He got an awful land in fairness. Started shouting things like: "Jesus Christ!" And "Oh My God!"

And sure that only exacerbated things. Everything was closed for about an hour. They had to send in the bomb squad and robots and all that to check his suitcase. There was a copy of the Bible and they somehow thought it might be the Koran and decided to nuke it. That was most of the hold up. Afterwards there was a smell like fried chicken and ashes and burnt plastic. And then the threat was over and everything went back to normal.

I waited until they were fully gone from the bar. Then went back and finished my pint. It tasted like satisfaction and the clearing of a blocked road. Conal's coke was still there too so I ordered another Brandy and mixed the two and drank it.

Next stop: London. Red heels. Thin arms. Layered brown hair.

Went through the security. Nothing to check in. Just had a bag with two shirts and a pair of jeans packed by Karen. Left the rest in the car. Fuck it. Eerie walk across the plank and in through the cabin doors. Gave the hostess my boarding pass. She smiled and handed it back to me. She'll be dead in six months. Car crash. Tonight she's very much alive.

The plane had the rattling feel of an old Ford Cortina, smoked seats and intense heat. The other passengers were drenched with Ireland. The wrecked side of a mountain look, eyes trapped in the misty reflection of constant drizzle.

Buckled up and got ready for departure. Then your man came with the drink. He was like a priest, and me there with my tongue out for the communion. I floored a few small Jameson and got drowsy. Head down. Drool. Fighting off phantoms that threatened like sobriety. My legs kept jerking with burnt out nerves, like they wanted to detach and find someone more compatible.

Stay where ye are, ye fuckers.

And then I fell away.

## *This is how I met Karen*
*Or*
*"The type of memories that turn your bones to glass."*
*Cold Blooded Old Times, Smog.*

Most Mondays I'd miss work and wake up around twelve. Look at the Westmeath sky out the window and let the fear grip, take hold, terrify. Some days there'd be a girl there, just as lost as me. A flashback of the night before. Singing on the empty street with a half drank pint and no taxis. Just guards and the busy chipper and the food wrappers rolling around the path.

This was how I met Karen. It was after Karma in Athlone. Her friends were all gone with other lads. She was standing against the window of the Bank of Ireland. She had no way home. All alone. Arms crossed, cold. I sauntered along. Been drinking since that morning. Knew her vaguely. Blonde hair. Black cardigan. Blue jeans. Green pointed heels. A necklace from her mother.

I asked her: 'Are you ok?'

'I need a lift home.'

'I've a car at my house.'

'Where is it?'

I pointed right, said: 'A small walk that way.'

'You're too drunk to drive, though.'

'That's true. But you can stay if you like?'

'I could. But you might get ideas.'

'Like what?'

'You know *like what*.'

'We can sleep in our clothes.'

'I'll take your bed, maybe. But you can sleep on the couch.'

'It's a start. Come on so.'

We walked through the crystalline night. The chill felt oddly warm as her scent caught me. I felt a bit taller. More confident. Less in need of a drink. Asked her: 'Can I hold your hand?'

'That'd be nice.'

Her fingers were soft, and delicate, and somehow familiar. It sent a rush through me. She said: 'Where's this place?'

'Just around here.'

And it was. We got in. Upstairs. Single bed but we did our best. She was shivering at first and locked around me. 'Keep me warm.' She said.

Then. Things calmed down and the water found its level. There was an unmerciful silence. The dark got darker. I wasn't sure what we were at. She was more conservative than the usual kind of girl I brought back. More notions. More morals. Deserved more respect. I was conscious of her hand around my waist. Her breath on my neck like strawberries. Our faces touching, frozen, poised on the cusp of some intense moment. Gradually, our mouths moved closer. Nervous at first. Then there was the corner of her lip. It was moist and sweet. Then her chin. Then her tongue lightly touched mine.

We lay like that for a while, just kissing, letting our tongues get to know each other. Eventually she pulled me closer, around her, over her, on top of her. I kissed her neck, her chest, her nipples. Undressed her carefully. She opened my belt and took me in her hands. Then in her mouth in a soft loving way. Going down on her was sensual, emotional, reactive. I found her clit with my tongue, like it was waiting, and massaged it gently. Kept it in place. Kept it interested. I knew I was doing ok by the sounds she was making, and the gestures, and the encouragement to continue. It tasted like honey I'd never known. She got wetter, more ready, her body began to shudder, spasm slightly. I worked my way up with light kisses until I could see her face brightly lit in the moonlight. Her hand on the back of my neck now, strong, persuasive, letting me know it was time.

The moment was monumental. A thrust, a slight fright, then a natural synchronisation of pleasure and rhythm and abandon. It seemed to go on forever and felt too short when it ended. She was still shuddering in the afterglow, as she held me, and I held her, and we held each other, and let sleep seal the deal.

We started seeing each other then. Drinks. Dates. The cinema. I was drinking less. Getting a bit calibrated. Next thing you know a year was gone.

Just like that.

It would always end up back at my place. One night we were lying in the bed, her head on my chest. Grey neon scene, Leonard Cohen in the background singing *So long, Marianne.* All worries vacant and empty, night coming down like opiate serenity. Then Karen said: 'I'm not getting any younger.'

'No.'

'You either.'

'No.'

'Laura got engaged last week.'

The calm coughed a nervous cough. Fuckin Laura. And that prick Tim she was going out with. Perfect couple. Mortgage. Big car. Wedding planned since ten minutes after they met.

I said: 'Did she?'

'Yeah. She's the last one left now. Of all my friends. Except me.'

'I see.'

'I don't think you do.'

'Are we not happy?'

'It feels weird.'

'What does?'

'Being my age and not having a ring on my finger.'

'Why?'

'People wonder if there's somethin wrong with me. With us. With *you*.'

'Fuck them.'

'It still matters, though. Besides. It's something I actually *want*. And my parents want it too.'

'They want what?'

'To see me happy. Mam is afraid I'm wasting my time.'

'You're not.'

'And dad is grumbling now aswell...'

'Let's give it a while. We don't live in *their world* anymore.'

'But how long do we wait? And what for?'

'Let me get some money together.'

'It's not about that. It's about...this going *somewhere.* Do you *want* it to go somewhere?'

'Yeah, just not so fast.'

'I can't wait forever. I want a family. A future. My parents want grandkids.'

'I know.'

She took a scan around, the single bed, the empty cans on the floor, my jeans and crumpled checked shirt in a sad pile. 'You need some direction in your life too.'

She had a point there in fairness so I said nothing.

Then she continued. 'We could at least move in together? Like somewhere...*properly*.'

I looked out the window. The stars seemed unsettled now, some chaotic buzz, stellar turbulence.

'Are you ok?' She asked.

Yeah, sound. I told her. Let's move in together.

'I'm sorry.' She said. 'Maybe it's because I'm late.'

'Late?'

'Three weeks. It's probably nothing. Happens all the time.'

## *Relieved English Bitumen*

Back on the plane. On the way to London. I woke up when the wheels hit relieved English bitumen. Everyone clapped. There must have been a bitta rattling, or they all thought we were in America. Maybe just delighted to be out of Ireland.

Then we all stood up and went nowhere for the next twenty minutes. Phones came on and made unnatural noise. I wanted to get sick. Then a woman turned around and said: 'Wasn't it awful about the bombscare?'

'Twas.'

'A priest that did it.'

'I heard that.'

'Tut tut tut.'

The plane doors finally opened, like a birth canal to escape. Got off. Stansted. The dominant colours were blue and red. What the fuck now? I considered options to the city.

There was an £8 bus or a £22 pound train.

I got the bus and bought a cheap bottle of red wine. It's all economics. The bus was called the Terravision. Would take an hour. Might be a good time to ring the mysterious Spaniards and get a feel for what next. I dialled and nothing happened. It just went: *Beep.* I left the phone down and thought about that for a while. Then it rang. I answered and heard: 'Hon yo?'

'John joe, yeah.'

'Yes.'

'Yeah?'

'Ok.'

'Ok, yeah. I'm in London. On a bus.'

Beat. He muttered something to the background. Muffled voice. Then he returned: 'Jon Yo?'

'Yeah.'

'You will come?'

'To where?'

He went back to the voice in the background again. There was a loud alert as my battery came under pressure. Your man returned: 'Citeee Yenter....?'

'Yeah, where?'

'Yenter.'

'Ok, where in the centre?'

'We will see you.'

'How the fuck will you see me? You don't even know where I'll be...'

'Ok, we see you.'

And he hung up politely.

Then the phone died and it started to rain outside and there was an awful smell of piss. I took the wine out of my bag and realised I had no opener so I had to use a biro to shove the cork into the bottle. It took a lot of effort and clenched teeth. Then there was a pop and a big load of it sprayed up on my shirt. I wiped it off and took a long drink that tasted like the leg of an old chair. Still, it went down well. Well enough to think about a few things. Like how was I going to find these stupid pricks when I got off the bus? But sure that was *their* problem. John joe has it all solved here in the meantime. Then I thought about Marilyn. And wondered what she wanted. Maybe she was in love with me? That was probably it. Only explanation. And sure it was all over with Karen now. I was sad and exhilarated at the same time. Like when you're secretly glad that someone is dead. You wouldn't admit it, even to yourself. Still, another drink there, Patsy, keep her going until the grief lifts and let the party go full swing.

## *Nesting*

Karen was a primary school teacher. She liked the sound of it too. Liked the way it rolled off her tongue in company. And her family were well impressed. It was all part of the plan. Up until we got a place she used to live at home with the folks. Pork chops and Coronation Street every evening. Nice car. No debts. Waiting for the ring. I'd call over and they'd give me the dinner but that'd be it. Wasn't allowed stay the night because we weren't married and we might go riding.

And now we're having a baby.

Imagine that?

They were all upset because we weren't even engaged. And they wanted a nice lad for Karen. And it was important he had a good job.

Which was a problem.

Because I worked in a slaughterhouse.

On the line.

Dead walls.

Dead animals. Smell of offal, like an infected sewer. Some men loved it. Had been there twenty years and knew nothing else. The red overalls were like full body tattoos. But I wasn't that invested. Just needed the money for drink. And I wasn't cut out for college. Just trying to be saving for the fuzzy future with Karen and the child.

The vet landed one morning in his white coat and Limerick accent. Said I wasn't sterilising the knives properly and why was I late? He hadn't seen me all morning. He was trying to make an example. Show authority. He picked the wrong man today. I was in bad form. Sick with drink. Poor hygiene. The usual. So I told him to fuck off and he took offence. Raised his arrogant finger and asked me if I valued my job? I answered him as best I could by throwing a sheep's liver at his head. And that was that. Got ran. I was halfway down the road before I realised I was still wearing all the gear. Apron spattered in guts, and a belt full of lethal knives covered in blood. But there was no going back so fuck it.

Then it was time for the dole.

Karen was delighted. She said: 'I'll just tell my parents you work from home.'

That went on for a while. On my own at the house. Cans, pizza, wanking all day. Soon the Social Welfare started giving me grief. They wanted me to go weeding graveyards and doing courses in how to use computers. Eventually the worst came to the worst and they cut me off. No money for cans. No pizza. Just wanking.

Karen was handy with the internet and found some site with loads of jobs on it. I saw one for *sales* and sent in the CV. Thought I might hear something in a few days. They rang me an hour later. Looking for someone dynamic, ambitious, hungry for a challenge.

I started the following Monday. Selling Broadband. Door to door. A respected industry. Revered by the Irish public. People showed their admiration by telling you to fuck off. Get a real job. Or mostly just closed the door in case you conned them into buying something. But there was no more slaughter. And no more vets. Out on the road with your *self-starter* attitude. No early morning alarms. Just clock in on the tablet at noon. Hit your target and go home. Suited me down to the ground. Plenty of time to sober up in the morning and time for a few pints at night.

It went grand for a while. Brought in good numbers and Karen was delighted. So long as she could talk me up to the folks during the pork chops.

He's the best in the country, she'd say.

At what? They'd ask.

Sales Manager, she'd say.

That *manager* bit was important. Just like when I was in the slaughterhouse and she'd say I was a butcher.

The mother bought it. The father didn't. He knew the likes of me. I was no more of a manager than the dog. He was hoping Karen would cop on and meet some pharmacist or solicitor or something. I knew the likes of him, too. I'd seen him at doors all over the country. Looking at his shoes, not knowing what to say, thinking I was some kind of knacker trying to flog carpets. And on it went.

Eventually Karen was twenty weeks gone and it was time to find our own place and wait for the baby. We looked around and found a nice apartment on Connaught Street. It was like a new start, new adventure. Access to all *amenities* which included a pub across the road.

*Nesting* they called it.

I liked the sound of that.

## *Scan*

Then. Athlone streams chiaroscuro. We were walking through Burgess park. Sun falls, light brown, and tender. Glistens on the Shannon like shards of broken mirrors. People sat on the benches and talked, or cycled, or strolled by. The resistance was soft, time was at peace, no panic, going slow. One fella working on a bag of cans. Parents strolling by with prams, playing the family game. Karen was in sunglasses and shorts, sipping out of a can of orange. The baby liked orange. We were sitting on a bench at the end. Wide expanse of brown gravel and Romanian kids on skateboards. We always came here before a scan. She liked to relax and talk for a while and enjoy the moment. It was a way to contemplate the future. When there'd be three of us. It felt like she was already here. Our little girl. We could feel her kick at night. A curious creature, eager to see us. Eager to be held, loved, adored and minded. Karen said: 'What time is it?'

'Two. What time are we supposed to be there?'

'Half.'

'How do you feel?'

'Nervous. This will be the final one until she's born.'

'I know. But they said everything looked good the last time?'

'I'm always anxious anyway.'

'It's just routine, isn't it?'

'There's no such thing as *routine* with this. Anything can happen.'

I looked around. The scene. The trees. The magical secret buzz. The lid of life's treasure box was open. Lighting up everything.

My phone rang. It was work. She looked at it, asked: 'Do you need to leave?'

'No. I need to be here.'

'We should start making our way over.'

'Let's go.'
'I love you.'
'I love you too. I love the both of ye.'

## She cried all night

*I'm sorry, folks.* That's all the nurse had said. It was enough. Karen was inconsolable. I tried to be strong but she resented me, like it was all my fault. She needed to blame someone, make sense of it. I kept hearing the silence, the terrible ocean of quiet that was usually a strong rhythm. I wanted to wait, maybe it was a mistake. Use a different machine, get a different doctor. Try something. Anything. *I'm sorry* said the nurse again. And she left the room.

Karen moved home for a few nights. I spent most of the time in *Vinny's* across the road. It was a place for lifers, dead enders, trapped souls in circles of numb hells. I was all three and something else, something more, something new and pure cruel. Cider made no difference, vodka made it worse. Jack Daniels brought on hate, vacuumed love, death in every passing second, killing the moments of life in between. Grip slipped, a slipping rope, through greasy drunk hands. The roots of a torn mind, the tree ready to fall.

Then her family kicked in with the Christian stuff. They said it was all our own fault. For trying to have a child and not being married. God's *way*. And it was obvious I was no good. Came from a bad breed. Nothing but a Traveller doing Traveller jobs and I was only using Karen for her good name and her money. And look what happened now? Would I not fuck off somewhere else? Then came the funeral. The plot, and the priest, and the burial and that tiny white coffin in the blistering rain. Haunts me every hour of the day.

Time went on but we didn't. We never did after that. There was nowhere to go. I wanted to try again but after a while there was no intimacy. She said it was stress. She didn't have the time. She didn't feel like it. She couldn't go through it yet.

Still, I'd try at night but she'd just tense up and be still as a stone. And eventually pull away. There was occasional affection when she'd have a few glasses of wine but in the end that stopped too. And soon she moved out to the next room. Said she needed the sleep. The space. And maybe her family were right? She said. I needed to *up my game*, aspire higher. Maybe I could drink less in the evenings? Her mother said nature can sense when something isn't right. Won't let the baby grow if the seed is bad. Could I not have tried harder to support her? How could I be so selfish? Did I not know it was all my fault, everyone knew it, everyone said it, everyone thought it. All the neighbours, all the relations, all the friends, everyone she talked said it was *John joe's* fault. Get rid of John Joe and find someone right. And now she was asking herself why she never listened. And now it was too late and she'd never recover. I was a disgrace.

That's how it went. Grief wrapped in hate. I lost interest in everything. The job. Life. Facing the day. Faking it. I didn't know who I was. Who I was supposed to be. Everyone else seemed to know, but I hadn't a clue. Like an actor that has played too many roles and lost himself. The sum of all impressions, but no real part in any. I'd pull up at an estate, or in some town, and sit there for an hour. Everything felt too late, like it was already over. No matter where I went, like a man turning up to a concert that ended yesterday. I wouldn't be able to get out of the car. Like there was a foot on my chest welding me to the seat. And if I *did* get out I could hardly walk, or knock, or talk, or care. I started to feel old, like there was salt in my bones, sanding out the cartilage, as if I was waiting for the sun to go down on my last dim evening. And I could hear a constant babble of people talking in my head. Mostly customers from the job. I'd lie there every night in the dark, feeling like I was in a crowded room somewhere, listening to them all raving. They were trapped in my mind and I couldn't get them out and they wouldn't shut up.

*C'mere and I tell you, John joe....*

*John joe?*

*Hey, are you the man that was here last week?*

*Sixteen she was.*

*Did you hear about that sad case down the road?*

*Where do I sign? Are you long at this? Is Athlone a nice town?*

So I started drinking on the job. To keep the babble down. Keep the voices quiet. Not sure exactly when it started. Think it was that place in Portlaoise. Warm pub. Carvery dinners. The phone kept ringing. The company wanted more sales. Higher numbers. The averages are down – we need *you* make up the difference. I was on the way out when I just sat at the bar, took in the smell of varnish from the counter and asked for a Jameson. Drank it down and the music got more pronounced. Twenty-One Pilots, *Chlorine.* It brought me back to a girl's hair when I was sixteen. The smell of it, and the dancefloor, and the way she held me and the cider and the nowhere. Just the moments, and her small tongue in my mouth, and how everything was obvious before it suddenly got so complicated.

I ordered another. Drank it. The song ended. It began to rain outside. Hailstones. The phone rang again. The manager. I didn't answer. Looked at my watch. Four o'clock. Blood stream ethanol electric. And a quiet mind.

## Clodagh

Next thing. Didn't I ride one of women at the Christmas party? Her name was Clodagh. Short hair and big blue eyes. Lovely Galway accent, like sympathy in a song. She was married but spent most of her time alone. Working for the mortgage and the hope that something might change.

She wanted kids, love, romance, any of the above. Her fella was a welder. She wanted to write books for children. The Broadband thing was temporary for the last six years. They lived in a big house in some place called Kiltullagh. Built on *his* land. She felt trapped. Told me this over the dinner. Pork belly. And Bailey's cheesecake for dessert. We were in some fancy hotel down in Kerry. Or Kilkenny. Or someplace like that. White tables. Five Stars. Open bar. Pink lighting that bounced off her wedding ring. One sure thing we had in common was a fondness for the drink. She was on the wine. I was on the double Brandy. And we were both well sloshed.

Later. In her room. She was more passionate than I'd expected. Hungry for the physical. Her tits bouncing in the shadows of the moonlight. Had that smell of my mother's cosmetics and ascorbic denial – like sweets you buy at a chemist. Either way, we were both mad for it. Both coming from a long drought. She asked me to tie her up. Put my belt around her throat and pull as I rode her from behind. She held on to the bars at the top of the bed. The silver moonlight came through the window and sprayed a light blanket across the room. She got tighter as I got harder. *Pull tighter* she said. And I did. She groaned, moaned, screamed and begged me not to cum. I did my best, but had to let go. It was glorious, wrong. I was seeing stars, like sexual diamonds, blinking brilliant, in the bright lunar lust.

We fell down exhausted, into the world lapsarian. Her face was flushed and warm. She was delighted to feel desired, wanted, complimented. There was generations here of lost passion, passed down through aeons of religious devotion and impenetrable damns of self-denial. She tried to tell me more about the husband. How he wouldn't get a sperm test. Said it was all *her* fault. Actually said she was *faulty*. And he wished he knew that before he married her. Said she was like a bad car.

And did I have ever kids myself?

I didn't answer. Had a pint of brandy and ginger beside the bed and took a long slug out of that instead.

And then she went on to something else.

Some lover.

Ex.

Hippy.

Would always have a piece of her heart. I was bored listening to her and I fell asleep. Puked all over the bathroom floor in the morning. Did my best with a towel but it was still everywhere. Bits of bile and blood and that fuckin cheesecake.

So I slipped away before she woke. On the way up the corridor my phone rang and it was her sounding confused: 'Hello, John joe? John joe? Where are you gone?'

I just hung up and kept going. Too embarrassed. Sank a fast pint at the counter and left for Athlone. Took me ages. Didn't know where I was. Motorways here, there, and everywhere. Phone dead, no Maps. Had to stop a few times and ask for directions. Mostly in pubs. And sure had to give them the twist while I was there. I got sadder and drunker as I got closer to home. Had I lost Karen? And after the baby, this would kill her altogether. I thought of that white coffin and cried a few times. Just let the tears well up and waited for them to pass. Quietly watched the grass go by and the sun going down.

Clodagh hasn't talked to me since. So it was awkward enough at work. I'd be up in the office. Picking up forms. And she'd be in the canteen with her cereal bars and her apples and if I walked in she'd just stare at the table and ruminate the food around her mouth.

Her husband came to pick her up one evening. Square head, black hair, broad shoulders. Driving a Landrover. It was sometime in March and the birds were singing and the streetlight was on but the sky was still Indian ocean blue. She kept her head down as she walked around to the passenger side and pulled open the door and sat in and said something to him as she rooted in her bag. Phantom smell of foundation here. And an image of a tangled hairbrush.

They drove on and I almost waved but then I didn't. I just kept my head down. I could feel him looking at me, though. Maybe she told him? New age therapy and all that post tiger afterbirth. Fuck, maybe it saved the marriage.

Anyway, I proposed to Karen shortly after out of guilt, and for the sake of something positive, and then I felt alright. Like the old me was over and I'd be faithful anymore. And it was all part of healing the wound, making an honest woman out of her. All that shite her family were into. Much as they hated me, they loved a wedding more. The mother be getting wet about the invites. The father looking forward to his big stuff speeches. And sure Karen was delighted. She dived into the organisation to distract her. And I became nothing more than a critical object to appear at the altar to make the moment complete. That's all I had to do. Turn up. Play the game. The closer it got, the bigger the event. And the celibacy continued. She still wasn't ready. Wanted to wait until after. Like that might make a difference. Stop the same thing happening. Less of a sin. Sounded more like her mother than her. And it wasn't like America where you have conversations about intimacy. Things just flittered away into a locked place and we ended up together but alone. And this big wedding was happening. And there was no way out. We were in a quare fix but I loved her all the same. At least that's what I told myself. But now I'm in London because I slipped up again with Marilyn. And sure that's not the half of it. Will ya c'mon ta fuck, bus.

## *The Hag's Head*

The Terravison stopped at Victoria Street and then went on another bit. I watched the London night through the window. It was busy with loads of foreign shops and black taxi cars. My blood felt like sandpaper and my stomach like it was full of caustic soda. Phone was dead and I didn't know what I was going to do when I got off in Liverpool Street. Probably have a pint somewhere. A pint of bad lager and watch some fruit machine's lights bouncing off the disappointed glass.

The place was called *The Hag's Head.* Can't beat the English for stupid pub names. Inside, there was a bald fella in the corner trying to tear bits off a starved chicken breast and there was a smell like mash and peas and sick on a carpet.

The barman was well kept. Black shirt and gaudy watch. Wanted to know my order. There was a whole host of ales in the taps but I went for a cider because I was feeling the silk hit of pectin. He left it on the counter and I paid and sat down. Listened to a thin woman with warts on her face give out to her husband because he didn't have a decent job. The husband was in a dirty white t-shirt and old jeans and runners and didn't look like he had any job at all. He told her to shut up and walked over to the poker machine and rammed in all his change.

I took a hit of the pint and looked around. Saw a socket in the corner and checked my bag for a charger. Fuck me, there was one there. Karen had packed it. Irish women, they'll hate you forever and still wash your shirt. I stuck it in and switched it on. It beeped with E-mails from *Donedeal* and work.

Work wanted to know where I was.

*Donedeal* had a cheap wedding ring if I was still looking for it.

I deleted them and listened to the voicemails. One there

from Karen. It opened like this: "Just to say – I think you're a FUCKING WANKER!! AND I HOPE YOU…"

I hung up before she finished. Not hard to see where it was going. Then, a hand on my shoulder, with: 'Hon you?'

I looked around. You can already see him. Half cast. Bad teeth. White shirt and a red tie.

I said: 'Yeah?'

'Come.'

'Will I bother askin where?'

'Now.'

'Can I finish my pint?'

'Hurry.'

I wasn't sure if that meant *drink it fast* or *hurry up and come on*. So I went for the latter and sank it back. Christ, I thought I'd explode as we walked to the door. Felt like an air balloon about to burst.

Outside, I burped violently into the cold dark of London. And there was noise everywhere. Sirens, buses, people talking rapidly and phones going and pedestrian lights warning everyone to walk now or get creamed. There was a sound like the blast of a powerwasher from somewhere I couldn't see. Kesheshsh. And I felt like I'd slipped into some more confident version of myself, a brief eclipse into who I'm supposed to be. And then it was gone, like a memory that never happened. I followed your man to a red waiting car. Some kind of Insignia. He pulled back the door and said: 'Sit.'

Marilyn was there waiting for me. She was all the women I'd ever known and still the one I'd been waiting for. I felt safe beside her, confident again, like the big hand on the clock of my life had clicked into one of its greatest hours. She was in a short black skirt. Jewellery. Long brown wavy hair. Demented perfume that put my balls on fire. She stared at me for a second and it stung my soul with obsessive desire.

'Thanks.' She said.

'Where we goin?'

'I'll explain later.'

'Are you in love with me?'

She looked ahead to the driver, like I'd said nothing, and went: 'Drive.'

Then she looked back at me and said: 'No.'

Great.

## *Song of the Empire*

Lights, the comfortable roll of wheels, the purr of the engine like the song of the empire. I put my hand on her knee and she brushed it off and said: 'Later.'

That brightened things up a bit.

I burped again. Held in a fart as best I could. We went through Leicester Square. All lights and Union Jacks and big screens and cinemas. I needed a piss badly. And my blood was getting rowdy for a right drink, starting to lash like angry lava, the insatiable bitch. Wished I'd bought a naggin at the airport.

The indicator went on and put my kidneys into a restrained gallop. We went down a thin street with cars parked on double yellow lines and there was a fella in a hood standing at the end. Then a big door opened in the wall and we drove in there. It was like a film where loads of gangsters meet and talk horseshit before they start shooting each other.

The car stopped and we got out and Marilyn started walking and I watched her figure as we went through doors and corridors and walked by offices with lads staring at computer screens. I let the fart go the whole way down and pure contaminated the place. And then we got to a boardroom. Big oak table and fancy chairs with wheels on them. There was a smell like varnish. Coasters and tumblers and water jugs and air conditioning. She said: 'There's a bathroom through the far door.'

Savage. I went. Serious relief. It was like Niagara Falls down the toilet bowl. They probably heard it all over London, like a microphone on King Kong going to the jacks.

After, we sat at the table and talked. What did she want me for?

'We need to wait for him first.'

'Who?'

'You'll see.'

'Will he be long?'

'He makes his own schedule.'

'So how do you know he's comin?'

'Stop asking questions.'

'Can I ask where I'm stayin?'

'My place.'

'Are you really a hooker at all?'

'What do *you* think?'

'I think…'

Her phone made noise and she said: 'Shsh….'

I looked around while she pressed buttons. It was dark through the tall windows and there was rain going slowly down the glass. I saw a socket and went to plug in my phone and she said: 'Don't do that…'

'Why not?'

'How do you think we found you in the pub?'

'Through the phone?'

She nodded and I said: 'Sure you've found me now, what's the harm?'

'If we could find you, so can *they*.'

'Who are *they*?'

'He'll tell you when he comes.'

'Can I tell *you* somethin?'

'What?' She said.

'You're a ride but you're startin to annoy me.'

Her phone went again and she said: 'Quiet…'

Bitch.

## Black Leather Pants

Your man never came. Whoever he was. We waited for an hour and then went back to her place. Apartment. Wood floor. Big bed. She gave me a serious going over. I woke up in the morning and thought about it and had to have a wank.

She was in the shower. London was outside. There was a radio beside the bed. I turned it on. Just in time for Reamonn, *Supergirl*. A dark underground beat, a lyrical triumph. The music played like a soundtrack as I walked to the kitchen. Geometric sun shapes. Found a big rack of wine. Red. Took one down and rooted out an opener from the top drawer. Found it under a clatter of knives and forks. I popped the bottle open and took a long swig. Vineyards somewhere. Long tall vines and perfumed afternoons. A taste of dry scented soil and serene potency.

Had no jeans on so my legs were cold. Turned on the telly and sat on the couch and scratched my balls. Wondered what Marilyn saw in me and then decided I didn't want to know. Because if I figured it out, I'd fuck it up. I'm a masochist like that. She landed out of the shower. I hoped she'd hop up for a ride but she went to the bedroom instead and got changed. Black leather pants, black shirt, jewellery. She shouted from inside: 'Aren't you getting dressed?'

'Should I?'

'Yes.'

'Ok.'

Found my jeans, then my socks, then my shoes. Doing the shoes was a sort of private ritual where I thought of a million things. Tying those laces. A girl I could have had in *The Piano Bar* one night. A dog my grandmother had that died from poison. Karen's eyes when I first met her. The nostalgic taste of her mouth when we kissed, like Carlsberg and Benson and chewing gum.

I stood up. Delighted the ordeal of getting dressed was over. There was a pain in my chest and I was seeing stars, like a head rush. Was fairly sure I had type two diabetes. Don't know how I knew. Think I saw the risk factors in a toilet one time and I was a dead cert for everyone one of them. Lovely. This wine'll keep me tippled now for the day. And where's this fella we're supposed to meet? Does he exist at all?

And then he knocked on the door.

He was old and decrepit. Bent over like the number seven. Using a walking stick. Marilyn made way for him. He walked in and I said: 'Hello.'

'Hello, John joe.'

'Not too bad now. You're keepin well?'

'No.'

He shuffled over to the couch. Sort of fell into it and sighed in pain.

'Are you ok?' Asked Marilyn. 'Can I get you anything?'

He shook his head. The king of all disparagement. Then he reached into his pocket and produced an envelope with my name on it.

'This is for John joe.' He wheezed.

Marilyn took it, looked at it theatrically, then walked over and handed it to me.

Naturally enough I asked: 'Is there money in it?'

'No.' Said the old fella. 'It's your letter.'

'I know it's my letter. My name is on it. What I want to know is where it came from?'

'It came from inside you. From inside everyone.'

'Musta been you that invented the cryptic crossword. What the hell is that supposed to mean?'

'You can start by reading it.'

'Be nice.' Said Marilyn.

I took a long drink while I tried to think. Nothing happened. I was in exactly the same predicament. Fucking confused. The envelope was white and thin and there was a small ramp from the letter inside.

I looked up at your man again and he was gone asleep. Head back, snoring. Like, what the fuck?

Marilyn said: 'He must be allowed to rest.'

'Fair enough, Marilyn, but what's goin on here, like?'

'It's your letter.'

'Can you do any better than that?'

'I got one too. In Madrid.'

'And?'

'It changes everything.'

'What needs to change?'

'What do you want to change?'

'It's too late for me to change anything. I've got diabetes two.'

'What?'

'Well I think I do anyway.'

'What the hell has that got to do with anything?'

'I might lose my legs.'

'Shut up, John joe, and read your letter.'

'I'm afraid of what it'll say.'

'You're afraid of a lot of things. The letter will help you with that.'

'What if I burn it?'

'Then you go back home, to your old life, or what's left of it.'

'Seriously, what should I do?'

'READ!'

And she pushed me back and slammed the door. And then I was in the bedroom. Somehow I'd always known it would come to this. That it would be just me in a strange room, staring at my feet on the floor, wondering what to do. I'd always thought the letter would be a gun, or a decision, or bad news that I could do nothing about. But now I had a choice and I knew it was going to weigh some heavy burden on me. Some responsibility or something. And I'm a lazy fuckin bollix so I didn't want that. Then again: What else had I for doing?

So I bit the corner and tore it open.

## Big shtuff

The letter was pure big shtuff. This is part of it.

*"...all that light, warm light, light like you couldn't see but feel, light that was inside you. So much light, that you are the light. You become the light. You cannot feel just one thing, but feel everything. You radiate, and inhabit, and become, yet stay the same. Stay who you are. But you are everybody. And everything. You illuminate the darkness, wherever darkness might be. You are the day, you are the sky, you are the soul. See that word? That four letters. That concept. A transitory thing. A thing difficult to grasp and nothing could be more simple. It is all, it is everything. This was He. This was Him. This was his teaching. You have seen him, too. At the corner of your vision. In the split-second moments you allowed him in. You have seen the floor of his chambers, you have heard the rustle and the crisp echo of wings, you have watched the blue universe traverse through time and you have heard the whisper of infinity.*

*This is where we lived. In this suspended always. This radiating brilliance. There was no time, no dimensions. Everything we touched and saw was reduced to a molecular level and beyond. Reduced to the unseen and the truly pure. It was a spiritual search that ended where you began. It gave no answers, just asked for obedience. It gave no power, just asked for loyalty. It gave no pleasure, just a flat joy. A constant hymn. A constant song of glory. It was that red poetry you hear in the choir of angels, trapping the corners of the soul and singing praise and love to...*

*The others couldn't handle it anymore. They wanted to live and not think about it all being a divine creation. They wanted to eat, make love, drive a car without knowing everything. They wanted mystery, they wanted ambition, they wanted adversity. There is only so long you can stay suspended in the forest of love, like a web of evidence, like a heavenly billboard, urging people to see you, but having to stay invisible at the same time. We are the photo-*

*synthesis, we are the transpiration, we are the life, we are the light, we are the mystery, we are the wonder, we are the instinct and the intuitive, we are the guiding hand, we are the answer you have been looking for but don't want because - what then? What is there left to know?*

*We wanted darkness, we wanted pain, we wanted ignorance and disease. We wanted an opposite, a polar reality. A magnetic other. So we rebelled. We started a war. We knew it was pointless. We knew it was hopeless. But that was the point. Wasn't it? To be in opposition. To be the darkness and represent the now and not the forever. To surf with you from one moment to the next and cause you doubt, and show you pain. To bring you love, and take it away, and make you rich to show you poverty. And to be alive ourselves. To be mortal, yet ageless, but to feel the yearn. To look up to the light, rather than to be the light. We created the moment, the now, the despair that keeps you sane, the sanity you desire but know that something other hides behind the veil if you dared to look, and think, and be honest with yourself. We created the will to live and to strive and to be greedy for life. Because greed is what drives you. And pain is what inspires you. We are the true music, the true lyrics, the space between the words, the understanding between the letters, the sum of the parts of the mind that always questions. We are your mind. We created your mind. We gave you conscience and free will. We gave you the power to overcome yourselves and not to simply obey. But to live in exile, to live in the corridor of freedom where you become who you truly are. Relentless, free, unaccountable. Your own personal divinity. Imagine that? You answer to nobody. You are not accountable to anyone. You do not need faith because you are certain. You do not obey an Almighty because you are greater. You are no longer blind. We have shown you what it is to be truly alive and yet you look beyond to somewhere else? Look now. Look here. Look around. You have transcended...you are the moment, you are the life, reach out and take it, the power is yours to bend your reality to your will...you have embraced de..."*

I stopped reading then. Tore it up and threw it in the bin and finished the wine and fell asleep.

When I woke up, Marilyn and himself were gone and this made me excited and I don't know why. I went for a shite and thought about what to do. I felt like calling Karen, just to see if she was ok, then I figured it would only make things worse for her. I'm a hero like that.

I flushed the toilet and went for a shower. After, back in the bed, I lay under the warm sheets for a while and watched the London sky through the window. There was the sound of traffic outside and people shouting and a city buzz, buzzing, like a buzzing city. After a few minutes I was bored and searched for my phone. I found it in my bag and took out the charger and plugged it in. I was thirsty too but didn't want to get up and go all the way to the sink to get some water.

Didn't matter anyway because the window smashed a few seconds later and there was fellas in balaclavas all around the bed. I knew this wasn't good, especially when one of them said: 'Get the fuck up, you're coming with us.'

'Any idea where?'

That's when he hit me on the leg with something hard, like a baton, and Christ, it hurt like fuck. I jumped up out of the bed and said: 'Hey, hey, hey, relax!'

And then they all joined in and beat me unconscious.

## *Before the stag*
## *or*

*"You are now about to witness the strength of street knowledge."*
N.W.A. Straight Outta Compton.


My team leader in the broadband job was a fella called Jack. He'd have to come and meet me every so often and fill out some forms. Safety audits or something. And then we'd do a couple of sales together and drink coffee from petrol stations. He was early forties. Black hair. Grey stubble. Played the game fast and loose. Had been doing this kind of thing for years.

Driving taxis.

Running pubs.

Buying and selling cars.

Bitcoin.

Today we were sitting in the car at *Corrib Oil* on the Ballymahon Road. Light rain. Athlone people walking around the place.

Jack asked: 'How's your commission?'

My stomach was raw from a feed of Brandy I had last night. I was using the coffee to wash down a bag of black puddings and hoping they might calm the burn.

I said: 'Fine. It's the bills that's the problem. Haven't sold much lately.'

'You can sing that.'

'Fuckin Karen has more debt built up than the Lehman Brothers.'

'She wants a nice day out?'

'She does. *Very* nice.'

He looked around, said: 'I know a crowd that's looking for

people if you're interested? Good money in it.'

'What's that?'

'Debt Collector.'

'Debt collector?'

'The legal kind. Lad like you be perfect for it.'

'How's it work?'

'Come with me tomorrow. I'll show you.'

'What about *this* job?'

'This new place be twice the wages and half the hassle. If you like it you can pack in this fuckin job altogether.'

'Team leader of the year.'

'Who are ya tellin? I'm doing it myself on the side for a while but I'm moving on to something else instead.'

I ate another pudding, looked at the rain, said: 'Sound sure. Let's take a look.'

## *Gangsta Gangsta*

I met him the next day outside Walsh's on Connaught Street. Denim Jacket. Americano. Smoking. People knew him that walked by.

Howya, Jack. All that. He saw me coming, said: 'Howya now?'

'Sound.'

'We'll take a walk down here so.'

'Where are we goin?'

'Battery Heights.'

We walked on. POV: Feet on footpaths. Dull thud from a car radio. Light rain, but cold. Jack's Benson, like childhood hay. We turned the corner and got into the estate.

Jack asked: 'What's the ultimate product to sell?'

'Somethin everybody wants.'

'Exactly. Does everybody want Life insurance?'

'No.'

'Home Alarm Systems?'

'Not many. Not enough. Most people want Broadband?'

'Broadband's good. What about money?'

'Money?'

'It's the ultimate, purest and most sought after product you can legally sell. You don't even have to *sell* it. People want it so bad - they come looking for you. It's more potent than any drug.'

'How do you *sell* money?'

'How do the banks *sell* money? They loan you a certain amount and require a higher amount back. Simple.'

'But we're not banks.'

'Not exactly. But in this job, you'll be acting the same. Same regulations, same principles, same criteria to borrow except we deal in cash.'

He kept talking. It was for people that didn't understand banks. They knew what a bank was. They just didn't know how to act in one. Our job was to go to their house and give them the money in a way they understood. In a way they felt more comfortable, more relaxed, less patronised.

It was a big hit with foreigners. But the Irish loved it too. Some didn't have bank accounts. Others didn't like bank accounts. Direct debits, online apps, low interest rates, all that was nonsense. They wanted to see the cash come and go. We got to the Battery Heights. Up around the back.

'Bit rough here.' He said. 'But good people too. You'll do a lot of business if you keep it right.'

'What do we do? Just call around and offer them loans?'

'You'll have a float. We'll get you that at the office. Say someone says they want €800 Friday - you call to the office and they'll give you a cheque. You cash the cheque at the bank, then go to their house and do the application.'

'Do they not need ID or somethin?'

He pointed at a house, said: 'We have a customer here today. I'll show you.'

We walked up the drive. Grass. Dog shit. Tyres. A shopping trolley. Jack knocked using the letterbox. It made a hoarse rasp on the weak wood of the door. Eventually, a man answered. Late fifties, grey thin hair, not very tall. He said: 'Howya, Jack.'

'Good man, Paddy. This is the new lad. He'll be taking over.'

Paddy looked me up and down, said: 'Another recruit. Come on in.'

Inside. Smell of damp clothes. Torn couch. Bachelor. News on the telly. Tobacco on the table. Some change and some medication. Last week's paper half open. Plates in the sink, unwashed. Old cupboards. Wooden squeaky chairs.

We sat down. Paddy said: 'So what do I need again?'

'ID. Proof of address. Payslips.'

'I have a receipt from the Post office. Will that do?'

'Twill.'

'And my driver's licence?'

'Perfect.'

'And a letter from the hospital.'

'No. Has to be a government letter.'

'Like what?'

'Tax, social welfare, anything like that.'

'Hang on til I see.'

He went upstairs. Carpet. Wood creaks on the roof.

Jack says: 'See here.'

He had a device in his hand. Some kind of Smartphone. Paddy's account was open. *Patrick Fennessy.*

'Paddy is lookin for €300. He had a loan from us six months ago and he paid it up so he's a good customer. I have the cash on me here. Soon as everything is alright and up to date we'll give it to him.'

Paddy came back, said: 'Letter from the Social. Will that do?'

'What date is on it?'

'November.'

'Perfect.'

Then. We went through the loan. A list of questions.

How much do you spend on electric. How much on rent, car, food, alcohol, beauty products and utilities.

The phone calculates the income against the outgoings and makes an offer based on what's left over.

Paddy's lucky. It offers €300. Jack counts it out on the table. Six €50 notes. Says: 'Same as last time, Paddy. We collect every week.'

'How much a week?'

'€20 a week for the next 26 weeks.'

'Perfect.'

Outside. Walking back. Birds sang, chlorophyll enterprise.

Jack said: 'Multiply €20 by 26.'

I did it on my phone.

'€520.'

'And how much did he borrow?'

'€300.'

'So how much interest is he paying?'

'€220.'

'Just like that. The €220 didn't exist anywhere in the world until we did the deal with Paddy. Now suddenly it's real. You get commission on your calls. Every time you collect.'

'How much?'

'10%'

'So when I collect €20 off Paddy I get...?'

'€2. But then €20 is the minimum. Some customers will be paying €50, others €100. They're the ones you want to take good care of. You'll have two hundred customers on this book. Good chance to make money.'

'Why don't they go to the Credit Union?'

'It's not somethin I bring up that much.'

'Still.'

'See Paddy there? How many people do you think called to him all week?'

'Dunno.'

'Not a one. No kids. No family. 55 years of age. Do you

think the Credit Union are goin to send a lad out every week to collect the money?'

'No.'

'And have a chat with him? And let him off a week if he doesn't have it? Or give him an extra day and don't charge him an unpaid bounce like the banks?'

'Right.'

'And if he went to a bank or a Credit Union he'd have to have an account. He'd have to go down and open one up. They'd send him back for the letter, or the ID, or the payslip, and then it wouldn't be good enough and he'd have to be going up and down and eventually he'd say *fuck it.* Much handier to have us come, give him time, let him find what he needs and give him the money.'

'And if he doesn't pay?'

'Not your problem. You're not liable. Just chose your customers carefully. Ask me if you have any doubts.'

'Sound. When do I start?'

'All yours whenever you want it?'

'Are you givin it up?'

'Yeah, but you'll have a new manager called Dave.'

'Dave?'

'Yeah, he's alright. Always talkin about shoes.'

'Shoes?'

'Yeah. It's fuckin weird. You'll know when you meet him. Anyway, I'm goin into a new thing with another lad.'

'What's that?'

'Poker machines. I'll tell you all about it again. Do you want this or not?'

'What about selling the Broadband?'

'Pack it in ta fuck. Call it evolution. You'll clean up here.'

## *Money for the hotel*

Did I tell Karen about the debt collecting? Did I fuck. Things were bad enough.

She wouldn't approve. And she'd tell her mother. And she *definitely* wouldn't approve. And her mother would tell her father. And he'd go fuckin mad. They were a bit like that. Think it was a social thing. Image, Christian, something.

So Karen still thought I sold Broadband and it was mostly the same hours so it didn't matter. Just better money. Most days we fought anyway. Stupid stuff, covering up the real pain. Throwing toxic fuel into a fire of grief. The game was blame, pivot off the problem, don't touch the source, don't look into the black sun.

I was on the way out to work when she said: 'Can you get rid of those knives?'

'What knives?'

'The ones from the abattoir. I found them when I was cleaning.'

'Where were they?'

'Under your bed. It's disgusting.'

'I forgot all about them. Sorry. I'll sort it out.'

'I can still see old blood on the blades.'

'I'll do it later.'

'Oh, and we need to put a deposit on the hotel.'

'How much?'

'€2000. Can you have it Friday?'

'Friday?'

'Yeah. They need it.'

'Just like that?'

'It's how it's done. And I'm meeting the photographer today too. She's supposed to be good.'

'By which you mean expensive?'

'Who cares?'

'Maybe the lad that's payin for it?'

'How can you put a price on this?'

'Because it costs money...'

'Be an asshole why don't you?'

'It's a lot of pressure, babe. That's all.'

'What do you know about *pressure?*'

'Two grand by Friday sounds like pressure to me.'

'Just get it from somewhere. You have plenty of money for drink when you need it.'

'What's that go to do with anythin?'

'Tuh.'

'Maybe we could split some of the costs?'

'Don't be ridiculous. I'm the bride.'

'Is your oul fella not supposed to fork out?'

'I'm not asking my *father* for money!'

'It's *tradition*...isn't it?'

'Not in my family. My dad says if you're a *real man* you can pay for the wedding. Time to grow up.'

Beat. I thought about the new job. It was commission only. No basic wage, just a percentage of collections. I said: 'I'm unlikely to have that money for you by Friday.'

'When will you have it then?'

'Soon.'

'How soon?'

'Soon as I fuckin have it.'

'But the hotel *need* it.'

'They won't starve.'

'They might let the date go.'

'Tell them to ring me and I'll talk to them.'

'I wouldn't let you talk to a dog.'

'What the fuck is that supposed to mean?'

'My point exactly. You talk like that to a hotel manager and they'll think we're a crowd of stupid rednecks...'

'Aragh go fuck yourself.'

'See? More of it! And did you get time off for the stag?'

'Yeah.'

'What's it going to be like?'

'Few drinks.'

'Where?'

'Dunno yet.'

'Who's going?'

'I'll ask a few.'

'Have you nothing organised?'

'No.'

'Of course you don't. Do you even *care?*'

'I do care. I want us to be happy. *You* to be happy.'

'You have a funny way of showing it.'

'Look, I know you're still hurt....'

'You don't know anythin...'

'Men are affected by it too.'

She scoffed. 'Yeah right.'

'I'm not jokin...'

'Could have fooled me....'

'I think about it all the time.'

'Just do me a favour and get organised.'

'I am organised.'

'Where are you going for the stag then?'

'I wouldn't mind somewhere abroad.'

'Like where?'

'Dunno. Madrid?'

'Really?'

'Yeah.'

'So you have money for foreign holidays and none for booking the hotel?'

I shrugged, said: 'Can't fuckin win with you.'

'Are you going to behave yourself out there?'

'Why wouldn't I?'

'I need you to be right for when you come back. There's still a lot of prep to be done.'

She made it sound like a school tour. I said: 'Sure isn't most of it sorted?'

'No. Not half.'

'Maybe calm down a bit. It's not the fuckin Electric Picnic we're doin. Keep it simple.'

'We're only going to do this once. I don't want *simple*.'

'God forbid.'

'Stop been a dickhead.'

'I'm not bein a dickhead.'

'You are. You're always complaining. Poor *you*.'

'I'm tryin to have an input.'

'Well. Don't.'

'Don't?'

'Yes. I'm doing fine without your negativity.'

'Negativity?'

'Leave it to me.'

'Haven't much choice, have I?'

'Nope.'

'You can't keep blaming me.'

'Why can't I? It was your fault.'

'Oh, here we go again.'

'You're a waster.'

'What?'

'You're a disgrace. No proper job, no money for the hotel, leave it all to me as usual.'

'What's this got to do with what happened?'

'Because I need a *proper man* and you just float around like a fairy, like it will all work out. We should have been married a year ago and none of this would have happened.'

'It wouldn't have made any difference.'

'We'll never know, will we? Mam said it happens to loads of people that aren't married.'

'It happens to loads of people whether they're married or not.'

'I'm sure being married helps, though.'

'You're just fuckin delusional now.'

'Oh, how fucking supportive of you!'

'I didn't mean it like that. You know what I mean.'

'I know you want to stick the knife in further because you're a coward and you didn't propose in time and you don't want to feel guilty about it. My father was right about you.'

'Oh was he now?'

'Says you're a useless waste of space and it was probably your weak seed that killed the child.'

'I think your family need help.'

'They're all I have with so little empathy from you.'

'We could try again. There's so many ways we can work together...'

'I want to get married. I want to conceive. I want to have

the child I'm supposed to have in the honest eyes of God. Why can't you understand that? I'm stuck with you now because it's too late to meet anyone else....'

'You don't mean that.'

'You have no idea who I am, or what I think.'

She slammed the door of the cupboard. Made noise with cups and plates in the sink. I waited for a moment of silence and said: "What happened to you? You were never like this.'

'I grew up. Maybe it's time *you did too*? And stop looking for sympathy all the time.'

'I'm sorry.'

'Just get out. And get that money for the hotel or else...'

'Or else what?'

'Or else I'll tell everyone what a useless dick you are. And how you killed our child...'

'Karen....'

She threw a plate of the wall. It smashed with all her violent rage. 'Just get the fuck out!'

Later, I pulled up in Sarsfield Square. Rain. Dog shit. Traffic. Feeling generally miserable with loss and buried grief. Everything looked shot through an ultraviolet lens, captured in an austere hue of emotional depravity.

I opened up the device. My hands didn't feel like mine, as if I was watching myself from over my own shoulder. There was a list of names and addresses. Work down through them. Call to them all. Collect and go home. Seemed simple enough.

My first call was a woman in the middle of the estate. She opened up the door in her pyjamas. Bloodshot eyes. Hair standing on her head. Voice like twenty Benson. She asked: 'Who are you?'

'The new lad. Collections. Money.'

'Where's Jack?'

'Finished up. Gone.'

'Serious?'

'Yeah.'

'Well I've no money for ya.'

'Why not?'

'I'm broke.'

'Your rate is €20 a week.'

She looked around. There was a few dirty coins on top of a degenerate phonebook on a rotten table inside the door.

She scooped them up, squinted at her hand, said: 'I have €1.73. Will that do?'

'It's a start.'

Sat back in the car. A wealthy man. Turned on the radio. *Lyric FM.* News going. Economy in trouble. Climate in trouble. World in trouble.

After, they let some violins sing, soothed me through Arcadia and into Ashdale.

There was a customer there that worked on a farm. Something to do with milking and machines and udders. He was making €780 a week according to his payslip. He wanted to borrow €1500.

Rate €85 a week over 26 weeks.

Commission for me per call @ €8.50.

Total amount repayable €2210.

Talking to him, he liked to keep things simple. Call on a Friday. I'll have the money waiting. No messing. Sound. I put it through and handed him the cash.

Thirty crisp €50 notes.

'Thanks.' He said.

And I left.

The bonus for giving new loans was €50. The incentive was to sign up as many as you can. Better still, if someone recommended a new customer they'd get a referral reward of €40. So often they were doing the work for you. Here, John joe. My sister wants money. Can you give it to her and I'll collect the €40 and you get the €50 and she pays the interest? Sure go on so.

## *The Shack*

I started hanging around with Jack a bit more. The odd pint. The odd game of poker. We'd meet up and go somewhere. Some house. Some party. One evening I was in Brawney Square and he rang and said: 'Do you want to go for one?'

'Where are ya?'

'*The Shack.*'

'Sound, see you in five.'

I was walking back to the car and there was a woman walking down the road. Not so much a woman as the kind of stunner you meet about every twenty years. Patterned yellow skirt. Knee high boots. Tights. A white expensive coat. Glittering earrings. Bright jewellery on her wrists.

Tanned. Huge blue eyes. Hint of gypsy maybe. Or South American blood. Her hair was ruler straight. Down below her shoulders. A scent like amber, rosewood, red wine on mahogany.

She was looking at me as I approached. Like she wanted to say something. A smiling scene of sexual voltage. I went for: 'Howya.'

'Your hub fell off your wheel.'

'What?'

'The alloy. It fell off your wheel.'

I looked over. She was right. I'd parked on the kerb and the hub had scraped off.

'How'd you know it was my car?'

Her eyes like sapphire, she said: 'Everyone knows everything around here.'

She never stopped walking. It all happened as she breezed by. And she knew the likes of me. Intoxicated. Helpless. At a loss with the sight of her. I had to follow, follow the dream. It was more of a compulsion. But when I went around the corner she was gone.

Later in *The Shack*. Jack asked: 'How's the debt collectin goin?'

'It's goin. Do you not miss it?'

'Not at all. I'm doin my own thing now.'

'What's that?'

'Bits and pieces. Poker machines mostly.'

'How's that work?'

'We install them in businesses and take the profits.'

'What's the profits like?'

'Pay the place €50 a week and keep the coins.'

'Who's over that?'

'Few local lads. They're into other things too but I keep it simple. How's your missus?'

'She's alright.'

'You sound miserable.'

'Stress over the weddin.'

'Is it still addin up?'

'Astronomically. Were *you* ever married?'

'I was. Not anymore.'

'What happened?'

'What happened my wife? She went mad. She's in the mental.'

'Sorry to hear that.'

'Don't be. I've great peace.'

'Did you love her?'

'No. Do you love your woman at home?'

'No. I used to. Not anymore.'

'So why'd you propose?'

'Long fuckin story. Do you want to come?'

'To your weddin? No.'

'I'm supposed to be havin the stag in Madrid.'

'I fuckin love Madrid. Great weed.'

'Do you want to come to *that* then?'

He thought, asked: 'Who's goin?'

'Nobody yet. I've nothin organised.'

'I'll organise it.'

'How?'

'The lads from the Broadband job'll all go.'

'Do you reckon? Some of them are sound.'

'They're apes. They'll go fuckin anywhere there's a session. I'll round them up. We'll get cheap flights and head over for the weekend.'

'Whatever. Something different.'

'Spanish women are lovely too.'

'I'm stuck for the *Best Man* aswell.'

'Jaysus. You're pushin it now.'

'How would ye be fixed?'

He thought, said: 'I'll do it. But I'm not puttin money in a card or any of that shit...'

'Sound. Just make a good speech.'

'You're cracked gettin married anyway. Take it from me. Especially if you don't love her.'

'Did your wife have a condition? Like a disorder?'

'She thought she kept seeing ghosts.'

'Where?'

'Standing over her at night.'

'Nightmares?'

'It was at first. But then it started during the day too. At work, on her way home, in the shop.'

'How'd she know they were ghosts?'

'Their heads would be fallin off and all that.'

'Oh.'

'Yeah. She tried to kill me one night. Thought I was a demon. And that was that. Ambulance took her away. End of story. That's marriage for ya. I've a new woman now anyway.'

'Do ya?'

'I do. Goin well.'

'That's good.'

'Tiz.'

'Where'd you meet *her*?'

'She's local.'

'Oh right.'

'Messy though.'

'Why?'

'She has a fella.'

'Married?'

'No. Just. He's dangerous.'

'What? Is he in the army or somethin?'

'He's in the entertainment business.'

'Showbands?'

'Poker machines.'

'Same as you?'

'Same fella.'

'You're bangin the big man's girl?'

'Yeah.'

'That *is* messy.'

'She's a ride, though.'

'There's plenty of others, I'm sure.'

'It might be love.'

'How dangerous is this fella?'

'Choppy uppy.'

'What the fuck does that mean?'

'He chops up people an odd time.'

'For what?'

'Stealing mostly.'

'Ah. You're fucked so.'

'Not unless he finds out.'

'Isn't that how this goes?'

'Not necessarily.'

'Still. I'd be worried.'

'I am. A bit.'

'Maybe she could just break up with him? And then down the line ye could hook up…publicly.'

'He's not the type to let them kind of things go.'

'What'll he do to *her* if he finds out?'

Jack's eyes went wide. 'I hadn't thought of that.'

'Now.'

He took a drink, looked around, asked: 'Do you want another pint?'

'Sound.'

He got them, came back. We drank. Savoured. Then he said: 'Her name is Rachel.'

'Where do you meet her? It's a small town.'

'Hotels mostly. They do good deals during the week.'

Beat. Then I asked: 'Is it decent money in the poker machines?'

'Works on commission. Comes in about €600 a week. Cash.'

'Not bad.'

'All in €2 coins. Pain in the hole tryin to count it. Reminds me of the days robbing the poor boxes. Do you want to do a line of coke?'

'No thanks.'

'I have some. Bought it off Rachel's fella.'

'What's his name?'

'Anthony.'

'Anthony. With the poker machines, and the coke and the lovely girlfriend.'

'Small world.'

'You'll probably have to emigrate eventually. Or get killed.'

'She might come with me.'

'Where would ye go?'

'England probably. Think she likes the drama. Feels like she's in a film or somethin.'

He took out his phone, pulled up a picture of her, said: 'That's her there.'

She was pure mink. Blonde, busty, big blue eyes. Indecipherable tattoos on her arms. Didn't look like the type to emigrate with Jack either. He took the phone back, looked at it, said: 'I'm meetin her later tonight.'

'Cool.'

'Anthony is in Belfast.'

'What's he doin in Belfast?'

'Pickin up a few things.'

'Poker machines?'

'This and that. You know yourself.'

## Mystical Chica

Back at work the next day. It was the end of the month so anyone with rent or a mortgage was making excuses for having no money.

Previously unmentioned relations were being rushed to hospital. Vigils being kept. God knows when we'll be home. Sorry about this. See you next week. You know yourself.

The council estates were in dire straits too. Oh, the bank machines are broke all over the town. Did you not hear? Could be a financial meltdown. And the Social Welfare cut the payments. And the neighbour owes me money and can you go and ask her? And I promise I'll pay you double next week.

More still sending out the kids to the door to say mammy and daddy were gone away for the weekend. And the top of their heads sticking out over the couch inside the sitting room window.

The chancers were in full force too. Some fella in Brawney wanted a €1000. I looked him up on the database. It said he had a loan before and it took him five years. The record-breaking bastard. So I rang him back with the bad news. He was thick as fuck, sounded like he was chewing soft rocks, said: 'Why? I paid off the last one.'

'You did. And it took you half a decade.'

'I was going through a hard time.'

'Sorry to hear that.'

'You sound fuckin heart broken.'

'Answer's the same.'

'Is that right?'

'Best I can do.'

'Better not show your face around here again so.'

'Why not?'

'Cos I'll break it with a brick if I see you.'

'Do your best, you fuckin gobshite.'

Beat. Then he asked: 'Please, can you not do somethin for me?'

'Aragh fuck off.'

And I hung up. Tough going listening to shite.

I did the count. Poor commission. Thought about calling it off and hitting the pub for the day. Then a woman rang, said: 'My daughter wants to sign up. Can you call down to her? She's good people.'

I will, says I. I'm doing fuck all else. The address was in Canal Walk. Down by Parnell square, around by Deerpark.

Pulled up. Found the door. Knocked on it. She answered. It was her. The mystical Chica that told me about the wheel the day before. Hint of gypsy. South American blood. Tartan skirt. Black shirt, gold necklace. Eyes bright blue and twinkling.

She looked me up and down, said: 'It's you.'

'It's me.'

'Come in.'

'I will.'

I did. We went to the kitchen. All done up. Newly painted. Most of my customers were council. She was buying her place. Mowed her lawn. No dog shit on the path outside. Whole place haunted by her perfume. This is what I'm talking about.

'What do I need?' She asked.

Proof of address. Payslip. Passport or driving licence. She went to the fridge. Tiptoed, size eight, maybe six. She found a shoebox. Opened it.

A big stack of administration.

Name, address, income.

Her name was Cathy. She had a good job. €625 a week.

Some kind of PR consultant. We went through the questions: 'How much do you spend on clothes and food?'

'€120.'

'Rent?'

'Mortgage. €500'

'Electricity?'

'€25 a week.'

'Insurance?'

'Don't drive.'

'Is there anything in the future that might affect your ability to repay?'

'Like what?'

'Losing your job. Leaving the country. Health issues…?'

'What if I'm already dead?'

'Are you?'

'In a way.'

Beat.

'Well as long as you keep up the regular payments then it should be fine.'

'Ok.'

Then I put it through the phone and it offered her €600. She was happy with that. I felt like she didn't need it, said: 'Something coming up?'

'No. I just wanted to meet you.'

'Why?'

'There's something I want to show you.'

'What?'

'It's downstairs.'

'There's a *downstairs* here?'

'It's a basement.'

'What's down there?'

'You have to come.'

'What if I'm busy?'

'It'll be worth it.'

'Is there a gang down there waiting to rob me?'

She laughed, took me by the hand, said: 'Come on.'

There was a squeak of the chairs on the tile floor as we stood up. A smell like bleach and vacuumed dust. Her hair was in a small ponytail and her hand was soft and made me sad, somehow reminded me of those early scans with Karen at the hospital.

We got to the end of the hallway. Light gleaming through the front door, refracting, bouncing off the patterned floor. The curve of Cathy's breasts through the black shirt. Her brown legs. We got to the stairs.

She bent down. Found a latch under the bottom stair and pulled it. The whole staircase came up. Lifted with a silent purr. There was another set of steps into the dark below.

'What's that?' I asked her.

'I'll show you.'

And she led me down. I was unsure as my eyes were trying to adjust to the darkness. Gradually the place lit up. Small lamps on the wall either side. Then we got to another door. It was big and awkward and had a wheel on the front like a submarine. She twisted it clockwise. It opened with a badly oiled squeal. Then she pulled it back and the hinges creaked.

We walked in. It was empty except for a red shape on the floor, like a pentagram. Some place for weird rituals. There was a skylight in the ceiling to the outside world. You could see the sun. And the sky.

She found a chair and said: 'Sit.'

I did. It was a bit awkward. Bit bony. Could have done with a cushion. My wallet was in my back pocket so I took it out and left it down. And my phone and keys too. She left to go somewhere. I sat there looking at the dust floating through the afternoon light from above. I was excited and curious and everything felt vaguely familiar. She came back with two leather straps and tied them around my wrists. It was tight but not uncomfortable. She had changed her clothes too. No more tartan. She was in leather now. There was a sweet smell as she sat astride me. Her brown legs were bare and she was naked underneath the black skirt. She opened my belt. Made sure I was ready to go before she put me inside her. Then. Nothing. She didn't move. I couldn't move. The chair was locked down. My legs and arms were tied. I was breathing fast. All my thoughts, emotions and senses were centred on one place. My mind was clear. I wasn't thinking about the job. Karen. The wedding. Life. I wasn't thinking about being tied up, or why. I wasn't even thinking about Cathy. Or who she was. I was centred. The whole of my being was in one place. Paused. I wasn't going back or forward. Just still. Stillness.

She put her hands on the back of my head. Pushed my face into her breasts.

She lowered her mouth, sweetly, lightly. Whispered: 'You are here.'

'I am here.'

'You are nowhere else.'

'I am nowhere else.'

'Do you want to cum?'

'Yes. But not yet.'

She moved slightly, just enough to encourage it, but not enough to bring it through.

'You are struggling.' She said.

'You don't know me.'

'I see you. I see through you.'

'How?'

'I know where you are. You are lost.'

She licked my ear with her tongue. 'But now you are here.'

'What am I doing?'

'Let your old self die. Let it fall away.'

'I can't.'

She moved slightly again. My blood was on fire now.

'You can. Just let it go. Everything is everywhere. Always. There is no beginning. No end. Just now. Just here.'

'Who are you?'

'I'm guiding you. I will guide you. This is only the beginning. We can stay for hours. Cum. Don't cum. It's ok.'

We stayed suspended like that. Could have been ten seconds or all eternity. It was hard to know. The fog in my mind had cleared. Like I could see my life from space. Full view of the whole event from conception to now. All the bends and forks on the road. All the smoke and fires, all the rare calm moments, all the war. I could wipe it all away with a brush of the hand. Take a decade between my fingers and crush it into pieces. Wipe it from all existence. It was all illusory, a series of photographs, trapped in the film of my mind, forever undeveloped.

And now it was all: Gone. All that mattered was the *here*, the present moment.

'Do you want me to release you?'

'I think so.'

'Into your new life?'

'How is it.... new?'

'Nothing will be the same now. I'm opening the door.'

'To where?'

'To your true self. You are a tame version of the man you are to become. Do you want to cum?'

'I want to cum.'

She licked my ear again. Hot breath. Erotic leather. Pulsating breasts. 'Ok, baby. Time to start again. Time to let it all go.'

She got into a rhythm. Sank down and took me deep, deep

inside her, then she leaned back and pulled my head into her chest again.

And then she did it again. And again. And I came. And came. And came. And came. And seemed to keep coming forever. And after, she was right. I was different. Some false part of me had died. Something unnecessary. Something surplus to requirements. The bridge back to my old self had collapsed and I was addicted to this new world and I wanted to do it again.

'You can come back tomorrow.' She said.

'Can I come back tomorrow?'

Yes, she said. You can come back tomorrow.

## *Traveller*

I got home that night and Karen was there making the dinner. I don't know why but I expected her to know all about Cathy. To have heard it somehow.

First Clodagh at the Christmas party and now *this*.

She turned around with a sullen: 'Hi.'

'Howya.'

This is how it went. Crazy fights. Tolerable calm. She hadn't straightened her hair and it was sort of wild and curly. Black jeans. White jumper. Still that cloud of sadness between us.

'How was your day?' She asked.

'Where do I start?'

'I'll tell you about mine.'

It was all stress about the wedding. And that bitch Laura. She had big ideas because she was the bridesmaid. All expensive notions that drove my head mad. Corkage, hotel rooms, honeymoons.

Karen didn't care as long as she could talk and not think. She was going a mile a minute. And this one rang. And this fella rang. And her mother wants this. And her father wants that. And did I organise the stag?

'Jack's doin it.'

Her face dropped with: 'That dodgy guy you work with?'

'Ah no, he's sound.'

'He's a chancer from what I can see.'

'No better man to sort a stag.'

'I just don't want you comin back with some venereal disease.'

I thought of Cathy, said: 'I'll do my best.'

'When is it?'

'Couple of weeks. He's bookin flights.'

'I think I liked it better when you worked in the slaughter-house...'

'It'll be grand.'

'And you still haven't thrown out those killer blades. It's like you're some kind of sick collector....'

'Fuck sorry. I'll do it tomorrow.'

'Ok, and you need to get on top of the stag. There's so much to do besides.'

'I will. Are you ok?'

'What sort of a stupid question is that?'

'I'm tryin to help.'

'Then you know what to do. Did you get the money for the hotel?'

'Not yet, no.'

'When can you have it?'

I got defensive, said: 'When I make it. It'll take a while. How's the teaching goin?'

'Don't be a sarcastic prick.'

'You're makin more money than me. That's all I'm sayin...'

'You want me to pay for my *own wedding*?'

'*Our* wedding.'

'You're a fucking pig.'

'Ok. Relax. It was just a suggestion.'

'Why don't you get the hell out with your suggestions?'

'You're pressuring me for two fuckin grand. I'm tryin to come up with creative ways to make it.'

'You're *the man*. This is *your job*. Can't you even manage that?'

'It's a lot of money to find at short notice.'

'Blah blah blah….my aunt Mary thinks you're a Traveller. Maybe she's right.'

'What?'

'She says there's a knacker in you. Is that what you're trying to do? Get my family to pay for everything? Squeeze us all dry?'

'Is that what Aunty Mary said?'

'You don't want to know what was said.'

'I'm sure you backed me up.'

'I ran you to the ground. Like you deserve. You need to give me an excuse to be proud of you before I say nice things.'

'That sounds like blackmail. Like you're saying "…give me two grand or I'll destroy you in public."'

'Take it any way you like.'

'Hard to believe I'm marrying such a cunt.'

And that's when she hit me. Slap across the face. It stung and stunned me at the same time.

'You're lucky to have me, tinkerboy…and don't you forget it.'

I was still working out a way to react when her phone rang.

Laura. Something about flowers.

I left.

## *Lost decibel*

The next day, I went back to Cathy's place but she was gone. I knocked on the door and there was no answer, only the hollow sound of an empty house. After a while you know when a place is empty. There's no sudden move of furniture when you knock. No shadows, no radio that gets turned down. Your knock is just a lost decibel that falls flat somewhere and dies like a sick invisible bird. I walked back up her path. The clean path. Out the gate and into the car. The car was surprised to see me, like it was saying: Back already?

I put down the window and let the Westmeath air sing and smelled the smoke that came down like a blanket from the open fires.

Cathy. What now? I kept working and hoped something would happen.

€500 to a Romanian in Monksfield Park.

€300 to a fancy woman in The Moorings.

€600 to a Polish blocklayer with brutal English but we got there.

I was going through the motions but I couldn't concentrate. I needed to see her. Them legs. That drug to nowhere. To everywhere. To the centre. Maybe she might be home? I went back and something more had changed. The garden was overgrown. The grass in the lawn nearly a foot high. The hedge on the wall was decrepit and dishevelled. The windows looked old and battered and didn't have the confident look from the day before. I pushed in the gate and the hinges squealed with rust. I looked around to make sure I was definitely at the right place. The right number. The right estate. I was. Except. *Everything* was different.

I went up to the door again. The path was cracked.

Cobwebs around the doorbell. I pressed it and it didn't work. Knocked instead. The wood was damp and cold. The glass rattled in the frame. I cupped my head against it. Tried to see inside. The only thing I could make out was a load of old letters and junk-mail on the floor. And a smell like wet timber.

I walked around. The living room was empty. No chairs, telly, nothing. Just an old fireplace and a lonely mantle with a broken clock. I stood back and looked at the upstairs windows. The walls around them were dirty with green scum and flaked paint. I expected to see her there. Looking at me. Like some ghost in a horror film. But no. Just bleak glass, and a drainpipe, and dirty gutters on the roof. I walked back to the car. Curious, confused, a bit scared. I thought back on how I met her. It was a woman that rang me. Mary someone. Sign up my daughter, she said. Maybe *she'd* know? I had to get her to sign the referral slip anyway. Give her the €40 and get my own €50 commission.

I went back through the phone. Found the call from yesterday. Dialled. It rang out.

Then it rang back.

Sound.

I answered and a nervous voice said: 'Hello?'

'Hi, I was looking for Mary?'

'Mary?'

'Yeah, I just need to get her to sign somethin for Cathy.'

'*Cathy?* What is it?'

'She'll know if you tell her. I was talkin to her yesterday.'

'Yesterday?'

'Yeah, she rang me and asked me to do a job for Cathy.'

'*Cathy?*'

I was getting annoyed now, said: 'Yeah. But it's a private matter and I'll need to talk to Mary.'

'I don't think Mary rang you. Or you were talking to Cathy.'

'She did. Sure I have the record of it here on my phone. This is how I'm callin back.'

'Is this a joke?'

'No. Why?'

'Because Mary died five years ago. This is her old phone. We kept it switched on.'

'Well....who rang me so?'

'It wasn't Mary anyway.'

'Someone rang me on this phone.'

'Why would they do *that*?'

'That's why I'm ringin. She asked me to go to Cathy's house....'

'Cathy's dead too.'

'No she's not. I had sex with her yesterday.'

'Oh my God. YOU'RE fucking SICK.'

And she hung up. What the fuck? None the wiser. More confused than ever. I looked back at the house. It was almost in ruins. There was no way it could have gotten that bad since I was there.

I turned on the radio. Five o'clock news going. Road crashes. Bad economy. War. Impending storms. Climate apocalypse. The usual. I started the car. Drove up to the top of the estate and turned around.

The rain fell light on the windscreen. I was shook but sure there had to be an explanation.

I thought back. Remembered the conversation with Mary.

Hello, she had said, this is Mary Green from 141 Village Crescent....

So I went there.

## Village Crescent

The place wasn't abandoned. Or old. Or run down. And it had people in it. And cars outside. And a dog barking at the window. Some little bollocks of a terrier. I knocked and a fella answered the door. Tattoos on his neck. Bloodshot eyes. Black t-shirt that was long due a wash. Yellow teeth, he said: 'Yeah?'

'I was talkin to Mary yesterday.'

'Are you the fella that's after ringing there?'

'I am.'

'Jane is upstairs crying. What did you say to her?'

'Nothin, just followin up a call.'

'From Mary?'

'Yeah.'

'Sure Mary's dead.'

'Well someone rang me from her phone?'

'About what?'

'A loan?'

He brightened up then. 'Do you do loans? I'm lookin for money.'

'That's not why I'm here today.'

'How much could you give me?'

'Nothin.'

'I had a job last year. I still have some payslips.'

'Can I talk to Jane?'

'No, she's crying. I'll have to go.'

He went to close the door and I said: 'How old are the payslips?'

'Last year. But I have dole receipts that shows I have somethin comin in.'

'They'll do. Can I come in?'
'Can I get a thousand?'
'I'll do my best.'
'Come in so.'

We sat down. The couch was a torn excuse for furniture. There was a fireplace packed with a plastic bag full of rubbish. A fish tank in the corner with no fish. A huge telly and a copy of *The Star* newspaper on the old coffee table. This fella that answered the door was called *Derek*. Old jeans. Acne. Smelled like the dirt between your toes.

I asked: 'Why's Jane crying?'

'Somethin you said to her.'

'She tried to tell me Cathy is dead.'

'Cathy her sister?'

'Is Cathy her sister?'

He looked around, found a framed picture beside the telly, picked it up and handed it to me. 'This is her here.'

I looked at it. It was her. Said: 'I met her yesterday.'

'Lad, she killed herself last year.'

'How's that possible?'

'I was at the funeral.'

'Killed herself?'

'Yeah, in the house. Nobody wants to live there since. Everyone loved her.'

'And what about Mary?'

'Gone too.'

'Someone called *Mary* rang me yesterday.'

'Do you need proof of address for that loan?'

'Yeah, but....'

'Hang on. I'll get it.'

He went upstairs. I looked at the picture again. It was Cathy alright. Tanned argan, sculpted figure. Some event, wedding, red dress and white high shoes and her hair down, behind ears adorned with shiny subtle crystals. And her blue eyes, superior to the lens, looking back into the soul of the world.

Derek arrived back, said: 'I've a letter from the hospital last year when I broke my toe after I kicked a bin when I was drunk.'

'No. Has to be a government letter, or from the Social Welfare.'

'Oh right. Will this not do?'

'No.'

'It has my name on it.'

'Still. Can you tell Jane I'm here?'

'Yeah, let's do the loan first, man.'

He found a letter from the dole office. Perfect.

Then. 'How much do you spend on alcohol and tobacco every week?'

'€120 on fags. Bout €75 on cans.'

'And what's your income?'

'€204 a week.'

'See, that's going to be a problem.'

'Why?'

'Where do you get money for food?'

'Jane buys it.'

'What about rent?'

'Rent allowance.'

'Do you drive?'

'Yeah.'

'Spend much on insurance?'

'No. I'm not insured. Can't afford it.'

'What if the cops catch you? You could lose your licence.'

'Lost it last year for drink driving already.'

'I see.'

'So can I get my money?'

I put him down as a non-smoker, living with his parents and having no bills. Doesn't drink or drive. The algorithm offered him €650.

'Fuckin hell!' He said. 'That's class. Can I get that now?'

'When you tell Jane I'm here.'

He went to the bottom of the stairs, shouted: 'Jane?!'

Nothing.

'Jane?!!'

*Fuck sake* he muttered, and started walking up.

I looked around some more. At the other pictures of Mary, and the rest of the family. They were all mostly bland, generic social clones, part of the same doomed blockchain. Extras in the life of Cathy, poorly imagined costumes and unsure of their motivation.

Then there was noise upstairs. Derek and Jane having an argument. Eventually she came down. Young. Thin. Blue dungarees and a red jumper. Black tights and converse shoes and big blue eyes. Long straight black hair. Her features were sharp and smart and somehow sad, like she had just been crying.

She looked at me, asked: 'Why are you doing this?'

'I'm just trying to figure out what's goin on.'

'How can you say you met Cathy yesterday?'

'Because I did.'

'But Derek already told you what happened.'

'It was her. He showed me the picture.'

'Why did you say you had sex with her?'

Derek said: 'What?!'

'It's complicated.' I said.

'Sick bastard.' Said Derek. 'Just give me the money and leave.'

'The money is in the car. I'll go and get it.'

'Hurry up.' Said Derek.

Outside, calm air, burnt colours. A white rusted gate that squealed. Cracked path. Car. I sat in. There was a smell like stale strawberries. Put the loan phone on the passenger seat. Hit the radio. A song by Twenty-One Pilots. *Stressed Out.* I turned the ignition. Went down the road a bit and swung around and faced her for home.

Derek was at the gate when I drove by. Gesticulating for me to stop.

I gave him a wave a kept going.

## *Who knows?*

A week went by. I thought a lot about Cathy. I drank a lot. The sky seemed dark all the time, like the light on the world had dimmed.

One day Jack came to me and said: 'How are you gettin on?'

'Alright now. You?'

We were in Supermacs in town. I was having a kids meal because it was cheaper than a snackbox and less depressing than going home.

Jack said: 'I've the stag organised.'

'Already?'

'Yeah, a good few of the lads are up for it. We'll go on the Saturday. Two weeks from today.'

'Massive.'

'Should be good craic now.'

'How are you doin besides? New venture goin well?'

He frowned, like he had a toothache in his brain. 'I'm in a bitta bother, actually.'

'What kind of bother?'

'The money type.'

'Oh. Do you need your job back?'

'I don't think that will do it.'

'Who are you in bother with?'

'Anthony.'

'The boss?'

'Him. Yeah.'

'And you're screwing his girl at the same time.'

'I know. She's a whore for the coke.'

'And you're buyin it off him?'

'I am.'

'And she's using most of it?'

'She is.'

'And now you're in debt with him because...'

'His girlfriend, my lover, has a nose like Harry the fuckin Hoover.'

'Will she pay anythin?'

'Like fuck. She doesn't even have a job. He won't give her anymore either so she's using me, to get it off him, to give to her.'

'How much do you owe?'

'Five thousand.'

'So the poker machines won't cover it?'

'No. I might owe a few bags of €2 coins aswell.'

'Jaysus, Jack. Things are bad.'

'They are.'

'Right. What do you need from me then?'

'What's your round like now?'

'How much am I collecting?'

'Yeah.'

'€6000.'

'Every week?'

'Most weeks. And with new loans it's going up all the time.'

'Ever see any danger?'

'Like how? Aggression?'

'Yeah. Or anyone try to rob you or anythin?'

'Not yet. No.'

'And how's things at home?'

'With herself?'

'Yeah, is she still pressurin you for money?'

'She wants €2000 for a hotel.'

'You'll be a while collecting to make that.'

'Would they give me an advance at the office?'

'Not a hope.'

'Didn't think so.'

'Everything has to be balanced and lodged every week or they'll have the risk officer out to your house looking for what's missing.'

Beat, he thought, then said: 'You know the money is insured?'

'Insured?'

'Like if you get robbed. You're covered.'

'Up to how much?

'Ten thousand.'

'Imagine that, Jack.'

'Imagine that.'

'Do you think I'm in danger?'

'In danger? No.'

'But you think I might get robbed?'

'Who knows?'

'*You* might know.'

He shrugged. Looked around. Young wans on phones. Obese types eating their problems.

'Just be careful.' He said. Then added. 'And smart.'

'Smart how?'

'Lads often have a compensation fund in case.'

'In case of what?'

'In case they might randomly get attacked.'

'How's that work?'

'However you like. Keep a couple of grand in your sock, under the floorboards, wherever. Some day you get robbed and you say the robbers took ten grand but maybe they only got eight. Who knows?'

'The robbers will know. If they get caught.'

'Maybe. But they'd have to get caught first.'

'Do you think that would be a possibility?'

He shrugged again. 'Who knows? Could solve your hotel problem.'

We let that settle. Then I asked: 'So where do you think you'll get the five thousand?'

'That's just enough to keep the wolf from the door.'

'What then?'

'Maybe get lucky. Do the lotto. Maybe emigrate.'

'Why not emigrate now?'

'I want Rachel to come with me but she won't.'

I took a drink of Fanta. The cardboard straw was useless so I took off the lid and drank from the cup. Ice cubes on my lips. Tasted like dry orange peels and salty water. Jack was agitated. Looking around. I asked him: 'Did you ever meet anyone called Cathy when doin the rounds?'

'Probably why?'

'I mean specifically. She had a mother called Mary.'

He thought, said: 'Doesn't really narrow it down.'

'Cathy lives in Canal Walk. Young, gorgeous.'

'I don't know. There was a girl like that there about two years ago but she's not there anymore.'

'What happened?'

'She moved out I think.'

'Oh, did she? Where?'

'Let me see. Something happened.'

'Maybe she went to Oz? Canada?'

'Yeah, maybe. Or....hang on.'

'What?'

'No, she didn't move. She....'

And then he told me. Same story. My heart grieved. I asked: 'Are you sure that's true?'

'Why wouldn't it be true?'

'I'm just askin.'

'Why are you askin? How do you even know about her?'

'Fella showed me a picture of her the other day.'

'Why?'

'Dunno, just tellin me about her.'

'So you knew?'

'Knew what?'

'You knew what happened to her.'

'I wanted to be sure.'

'Why?!'

'Because I met her.'

'When? Years ago?'

'No. Last week.'

'What?'

'I met her last week.'

'How's that possible?'

'I don't know. That's why I'm wonderin about her.'

'You mean you met someone that *looked* like her?'

'I was in her house.'

'The house is derelict.'

'I know.'

'So what were you doin in her house?'

'I signed her up for a loan.'

'What the fuck're you sayin?'

'Her mother Mary rang me and...'

'Sure she's dead too!'

'So I'm told.'

Five second stare, looking for the joke, then he said: 'You're one sick puppy.'

'Maybe I'm wrong.'

'You're definitely wrong. This is like some shite my wife would be talkin...'

'Ok. Forget about it.'

He looked at his watch, said: 'I have to go.'

'Where?'

'Coke. Gambling. Affairs. You be careful in the meantime.'

'How long do you think I need to be careful for?'

'Who knows?'

And he left.

## *Moneybox*

That night I got home and Tim and Laura were there. I could hear their voices from the hall. Laura was telling some story about meeting cops at a checkpoint and them letting her go. Tim was backing her up saying it was because it was a new car and they didn't suspect her of anything.

Karen was asking excited questions. *And what did they say? And was it a woman guard or a man guard? And where did it happen? And were you on the phone?*

I walked in and they all went quiet. Like they'd been talking about me.

Tim, big teeth, short hair, suit, musky aftershave, said: 'Hey, John joe.'

'How's Tim?'

'Hiya.' Said Laura. Blonde, cream skirt, fake tan, sparkling ring on her finger.

'Howya, Laura.'

Karen, crazy bitch, said: 'How was work?'

'Good.'

'Karen says you're booking the hotel this week?' Said Tim.

'Workin on it.'

'Better get it sorted.' Said Laura, all concerned. 'I've heard horror stories where people send out the invites and then lose the date.'

Tim chimed in with: 'Or the fella says it's booked and it's not at all cos he spent the money on gambling...or drink.'

'I'm sure that won't happen.' Said Karen.

'Of course it won't. I can't wait, I'm so excited!' Said Laura. 'Did I tell you the flowers from Holland are arriving on Monday....?'

Karen said: 'Wow!'

'When's Madrid?' Asked Tim.

'Next week.'

'Savage.'

And I walked out. Went to the bedroom. Noticed the knives still under the bed. Fuck, still hadn't done that. They were tucked into the butcher's belt I brought home that day I got fired. Not sure why I even kept them. Wasn't fucking nostalgia anyway. Made a mental note to throw them away in the morning.

I had a small steel box where I could store some cash if I had too much to carry around. I took it out. Opened it. Put the money from the day inside. Then I noticed a space under the wardrobe. It was blocked off by a wood panel. I kicked it and it gave way. I tried the box and it fitted perfectly. Then I put the panel back. I'd leave half the collections there every evening from now on. And if I got robbed out in the street, that'd be my compensation.

Like Jack said: Who knows?

## *Stag*

Stag coming up. Up and coming. Bounce goes the bounce over the Athlone bridge. River Shannon breathes like the mother of eternity. Traffic buzzards, buzzing, time like dissipating droplets disappearing, one after another, after another. I had a naggin in the glovebox. Jameson. Supped on that. Let the radio chime, chime with the engine, and the engine with the road and the road going to nowhere that meant anywhere. Whisky bites and glows, oils up the machine. Ready to conquer another unconquerable day. Thoughts of getting on a plane. Out of the country. I was up for it, like the gates of Alcatraz were set to open.

Jack had eight lads lined up. I knew most of them. They were all able to drink and have the craic. One of them used to live in Madrid and knew the best places to go. That sounded good. I looked around. The sky was mostly grey. Grey Ireland. Grey Athlone. A smoky pallor, like mist you can't see.

My wipers were old and squeaked and squalled when they went back and over the windshield. Phone ringing with people looking for money. Needing money. Money for life, money for love, money for food, money for medicine, money for paint, money for the sake of having money. Business was starting to build up. Referrals, new doors, quality collections. I was making money selling money. Real money. But some days a song would catch me, pull me somewhere, and I'd think I'd never come back. Just for a second. I'd see the far side. The gravitational pull on the spirit. That tiny coffin. And some nights I dreamt of Cathy. We'd be in her house again. And I'd be signing her up but it would be like I'd known her for years. Known her forever. Like we were married or something. Real married. Not the Beef&Salmon job. More like we loved each other and the wedding was an afterthought. Not a hope it would make things alright. I'd feel safe around her. And I'd be asking her the stupid questions about her income or whatever but really I'd just want to bring her to a bedroom somewhere. It was the way things were supposed to be with Karen. Before everything went wrong. Before the lost dream.

The phone rang. I looked at the screen. An unfamiliar number. I answered and a man said: 'Hello, John joe?'

Hoarse voice. Alex Higgins type. Dead background. No noise, like a soundproof room.

I said: 'Yeah?'

'Are you the man that does the money? The Jewman?'

'Who's askin?'

'I got your number from a neighbour of mine.'

'What do you want?'

'I'm lookin for €2000.'

'Were you with us before?'

'A couple of years ago.'

'What's the name?'

'Paddy Considine.'

'How's the credit rating?'

'Good, I paid everything back.'

'We'll need some details.'

'I have everythin.'

'ID, Payslips, Proof of Address?'

'All here.'

'When do you need it?'

'When can you do it?'

'Friday/Saturday?'

'Could you do Friday? I'm a bit stuck.'

'I'll try. What's the address?'

'96 Oak Park Drive. Out by the college. Can you be there at three o'clock?'

'I'll let you know.'
'I'm badly stuck now.'
'Sound'
'Will you be there Friday at three so?'
'I'll do my best. No guarantees.'
'I'll be waiting.'
And he hung up.
€2000. Weekly payment of €120.
€12 a collection. Lucrative.

## *Complaint*

After Jack quit I had to report to a different manager. His name was Dave and he was happy because I was making good money, putting in long hours, dodging the house, and the toxic fights with Karen.

He met me one day in *The Creggan*. Long black coat and some kind of expensive jumper and a scarf. Big car. SUV. Far cry from my own Vectra. I was sitting in the corner when he walked in, saw me, mimed: 'Coffee?'

'Go on so.'

He got them and sat down. A year from now he'll be dead. An undiagnosed heart defect from birth. He'll go asleep and won't wake up. Figure that. Today he's very much alive. Buying the coffees. He sat down. Styrofoam cup. Two sugars. I put them in. Stirred. Took a sip. Caffeinated world. Sharper. More alert.

'You're doin great.' He said.

'Not too bad.'

'Collected six grand last week and five new doors. I'd say better than *not too bad*.'

'I like the work.'

'That's good.'

'All ok on your side?'

'A complaint came in actually. That's why I called.'

'A complaint? From who?'

'A man called Derek?'

'Oh.'

'You remember him?'

'I do.'

'Says you offered him €650 and then didn't come back?'

'There was more to it than that.'

'Do you want to explain?'

'He was aggressive so I needed to say anythin I could to get out of the house.'

'Well he rang head office and they're not happy.'

'I was concerned for my personal safety.'

'They're concerned for their bottom line. You know how it goes.'

'I do. Either way I reckon he'd be a bad payer.'

'Did anythin else happen?'

'Hmm…no. Why?'

'He made some…odd allegations.'

'Like what?'

'Something about sleeping with dead people?'

'Oh….'

'Obviously there's no truth to that. He must be on something.'

'Yeah. Like…LSD.'

'Anyway, I've talked them down at headquarters and you don't have to sign him up if you don't want to. Just be careful.'

'I will.'

'Be smart.'

'Ok.'

'Let me see, what else? I'll need to do some calls with you. Just for observation.'

'No problem. Where would you like to go?'

'Not today. I'm busy. I need to buy new shoes.'

'Shoes?'

'Yes, there's a sale on in town.'

'Oh.'

'Have you any loans comin up this week?'

'I just got a call for one.'

'How much?'

'€2000. Friday.'

'Great. I'll come along. Have you got the cheque at the office yet?'

No. I'll do that tomorrow.'

'Do. See you Friday.'

He took off. I stuck around for a few minutes. Let the sky settle, let the calm clouds float, let the cars come and go. It was going to be a busy evening. I threw back another coffee. It was some kind of fancy shite but I didn't care as long as it did the job. Then the phone rang. I answered. A woman's voice. High pitched, like a parrot under pressure. 'Hello, are you The Jewman?'

'Who wants to know?'

'Can you give me €2000?'

'Who are you?'

'This is Ciara Lynch.'

'Did I meet you before?'

'I don't think so. I live in Oakwood Park.'

'Oakwood park?'

'Yeah, do you know it?'

'What number?'

'90. My neighbour Paddy Considine said you're doin a loan for him on Friday. I want one too.'

'And you want €2000?'

'Yeah, I'm a good payer.'

'Were you with us before?'

'No.'

'So how are you a good payer?'

Pause, then: 'Whaaaaa....?'

Someone said something in the background. The she said: 'I was with a different company and I paid them all back. Can you meet me on Friday? Same time as you're doing Paddy's loan?'

Could be handy. Two loans in the one spot. I said: 'What's your name?'

'Ciara I told ya.'

'Ok, Ciara. Are you workin?'

'I am. In the hospital.'

'What do you need the money for?'

'Turf.'

'That's a lot of turf?'

'Oh, and the car broke.'

'Hmm....we'll put you through the system and see what it offers.'

'I really need €2000.'

'I'll do my best.'

'Can you come on Friday so?'

'Maybe.'

'Please.'

'I'll ring you Thursday evening.'

'Please do. Cos I can't get around. And I need the turf.'

'Ok.'

'Ok. By bye bye bye bye by bye....thanks.'

And she hung up.


That night, driving home, I pulled in at *Vinny's* on Connaught Street. Pushed open the door and Harry the local alky was playing air guitar in the middle of the floor. *Black Sabbath* were on the jukebox. Imagine that? They still had a jukebox. Harry was giving it all the magical chords.

I sat at the bar. There was a young blonde girl working. Few lifers along the counter solving problems. The economy. Religion. Politics. I drank a fast whisky. Settled the shakes. Then the phone rang. I said: 'Hello?'

A voice like Dublin impatience. 'Hello, can you give me €5000.'

'Who's this?'

'This is John.'

'John who?'

'John Kelly.'

'Did I meet you before?'

'No. Can I have the money?'

'There's a process, John.'

'A wha?'

'An application.'

'My friends in Oakwood said you'd give it to me?'

'What friends?'

'Paddy and Ciara. Said you're givin them money Friday.'

'I can try, but I can't guarantee you'll get it. Are you workin?'

'I'm on a scheme.'

'How much do you make a week?'

'The usual.'

'What's the usual?'

'€204.'

'And you want €5000?'

'I do a bit on the side too. Painting mostly.'

'Do you get payslips?'

'No. Cash. Can you give me the €5000?'

'No.'

Beat. Then: 'Whaaa…?'

'We can try €2000 maybe.'

'Can you give me that?'

'We'll try. Have dole receipts, ID, and Proof of Address ready.'

'Ok. When will I know?'

'If you got it?'

'Yeah.'

'We'll give you an answer on the day.'

'Oh, so you'll have the cash on ya?'

'If your loan works out.'

'That's grand so. Can you come Friday?'

'How's three o'clock?'

'That'll do. Good man.'

And he hung up. I checked the time. Almost half nine. Karen would hardly be in bed yet. I ordered a pint of Bulmers. *Sweet Child of Mine* on now. Harry really getting into it. The cider arrived. I crippled it. Let the music in, wash over me, all the way to the magnetic nerves.

## *Yvette*

When you needed money you went to an office on the Dublin road. You had to go out by the Golden Island roundabout. And there was *Tubs&Tiles* and some kind of furniture shop on the right. It was the college area too so there was a lot of students around.

Took a right after Valley Court and there it was. Above a place that used to be an Indian restaurant. The old sign was still there.

*Bombay Grill.*

I pulled up outside. There was a good song on the radio so I let it run for a couple of minutes. Not sure who it was. And the DJ didn't say the name when it was finished. Fuckin hate that. Then. I walked in. Up a stairs. Through a door. Smell like wet clothes and torn lino on old floors. Each step creaked and echoed. Echoed and creaked. Wood from the cut trees, singing on the dead corridor walls.

And the wallpaper was tattered, and green, and the bits still left were trying to cover a stone cold grey masonry that dared you to try and outlive it.

I got to a big white door. Made of something cheap, like matchsticks glued together and covered in white paint. I pushed down the gaudy handle and it opened with a squeal.

Inside. Fax machines. Large cabinets. Oak tables. Folders. A whiteboard on the wall with some inspirational quotes. The sun was a yellow shadow, bouncing off the carpet. Particles like dusty angels, floating through the ancient finance. The woman that did the cheques had glasses that hung around her shoulders. She used ballpoint pens and liked to keep things exact.

Her name was Yvette. Late sixties. Maybe seventies. She's going to live until she's one hundred and five years old. Today she's very much alive.

She looked up, said: 'John joe?' Like she didn't approve of me at all. Had seen the likes of me come and go and felt it would end bad.

'Yvette.'

'You need a cheque, I presume?'

'I do.'

'How much?'

'Seven Thousand.'

'Busy week ahead?'

'Seems like it.'

'Are they new or existing customers?'

'All new.'

'How many?'

'Three. New customers. New doors.'

'Trustworthy?'

'We'll find out, I suppose.'

'Employed?'

'Two of them are. One is on a scheme.'

'*Scheme*....how much does *Mr. Scheme* want?'

'Five thousand.'

'You must be joking?'

'I'll chance him for two.'

'Hundred I hope? Not two thousand, surely?'

'Sure isn't this the business we're in?'

'Did he sound reliable?'

'Yeah.'

'Defaulters don't look good, you know?'

'I do. Can I have the cheque now?'

She pursed her lips. 'How much did you say?'

'€7000.'

She went to a filing cabinet. Opened it up. Pulled up a folder with forms inside it. Took out a sheet. Handed it to me, said: 'Write down their names here.'

I did. Then she got the chequebook. Wrote it out. Asked me to sign the back of it. 'At least you're growing the agency.' She said.

'Yeah.'

'Where do you usually cash cheques?'

'Here in town.'

'At the bridge?'

'Yeah.'

'Ok, it's a lot of money. Just be careful.'

'I will.'

'When are you doing the loans?'

'Friday.'

'All on the same day?'

'Three referrals. Same area.'

'Is anyone going with you?'

'Dave is due to do a couple of visits with me.'

'That would be wise.'

'I'm sure there's nothin to worry about.'

'Who knows?'

After, I went to the bank. It was busy. Dominant colour was pink. Thick glass at the counter. Queue of people waiting. All on phones, killing time, time being killed. Nobody talking. People afraid to talk. There was a fella in front of me with a lodgement from *Paddy Power* and it took ages.

There. They asked for my licence. My address. My signature. Then handed me €7000 cash in a white envelope. I said thanks and walked out. Through the back door and into the carpark. There was a slight drizzle and people were trying to park and making a bollix of it.

I walked down the steps and over to the Vectra. There's always a moment when you're walking to the car and you have the envelope full of money and someone could easily rob you. I got more conscious of it after the chat with Jack. But today nothing happened. I sat in. Turned the ignition. Radio came on with Little Green Cars - *Clair de Lune.* Pure soundtrack. Brought me nicely over the bridge.

## Actual Cash

Back at the house. Took out the money.
*It broke down like this:*
€3000 for John Kelly
€2000 for Ciara Lynch
€2000 for Paddy Considine.
**Sum Total:** €7000

I put it under the wardrobe and went off to work. Did the usual rounds.

Priory Park. Church Hills Road. The Glen. Cloughanboy. Mayfield Grove.

Most people were home and had money ready so it was looking like a decent day. The Mayfield crew were a strange one. Intelligent people, respectable jobs, but no financial IQ. If they went to the Credit Union they'd be paying 8% per cent interest. When they borrowed with me it would be 195% but they didn't know the difference.

Or they didn't care.

Or they liked the idea of some fella calling and doing it all for them. Either way, it was good money and I wasn't complaining or giving them advice. It was only two o'clock and I had €1500 collected already. I was in Bloomfield Drive when Jack rang, shaky voice, said: 'All set for Saturday?'

'Yeah. What time are we goin?'

'Have to be at the airport at 10am. Leave our stuff at the hotel at two o'clock and then on the piss for the weekend.'

'Sounds fuckin lovely. How are we payin for the rooms?'

'I'll collect it off the lads and sort it. We'll cover yours too.'

'Why? I'll pay myself.'

'Fuck that. It's *your stag*. Leave it to me. Least we could do. Will you be wrapped up with the money job by then?'

'The collecting?

'Yeah.'

'Should be. I've a few loans Friday and I'll do the collections and fuck it after that.'

'Good man.'

'You ok, you sound nervous?'

'Just lookin forward to gettin out of dodge for a couple of days.'

'How's the Anthony situation?'

'Not great. I bought a bit of cryptocurrency and hoping it'll swing upwards.'

'Anythin more certain?'

'There's a good horse runnin Friday, and I did the EuroMillions, so surely somethin has to give.'

'Surely. How's Rachel?'

'Flat out sniffing coke.'

'Trouble in paradise?'

'Far from paradise we are these days.'

A call came in. I looked at it, said: 'Dave's ringing me here.'

'The manager?'

'Yeah. He wants to meet me Friday.'

'Why?'

'Observation for a loan or somethin.'

'Tell him to fuck off. Himself and his fancy shoes.'

'I'll go.'

Jack hesitated. Like he was about to say something, then said: 'Sound.'

## Grey Goose

Friday came. I had €7000 collected. A lot of customers were coming good and the old ones were paying up because they wanted more credit and had to pay off the existing balance first. The plan was to do the three new loans. I'd use the €7000 from the collections and leave the cash from Yvette at the house.

No point carrying it around. Who knows?

The suitcase was packed for the stag. The thirst was in. I had a flask full of Grey Goose to keep me tippled. Took a long wallop as I drove by the cop station. Turned left at the AIB and right towards the town centre. I rang John Kelly on the way. Said: 'I'm on the way over.'

'Now?' He said.

'Yeah, I'm at St.Hilda's.'

'Oh right….and eh…have ya the money?'

'I do. Get your stuff ready.'

'Sound, sure. I'll see you here. Paddy and Ciara are here too. You know that sure? We're all gettin the money together.'

'Yeah, that'll do.'

Click.

The world had a warped, prism look. Sort of a cubist slant to all the houses, the way the light bounced off the glimmering windows. Bit like you were looking at things through a liquid bubble. And one of my hands felt bigger than the other. My right hand was like it was big and awkward and clubbed and my left seemed awful far away. And all the cars looked like they were made of weak paper. Like you could crash into them and nothing would happen, just a loud tear and you could keep going. I narrowly missed a pedestrian on Grace Park Road. She gave me a funny look, like I was a bit mad, or drunk or something. Imagine that?

Dave the manager was already waiting. I pulled in beside him. Made sure I had all the money. Took a long wallop of the vodka and walked over.

Hopped in. Onboard computer. Clean dash. Bin full of receipts and apple cores. Smell like leather and laces. The back seat littered with shoeboxes.

He said: 'How's the high roller?'

'Good now. Good.'

'So where are these guys?'

'The first one is 96. But we can do the other two there too. They're all friends.'

'Nice. Let's do it, sire. Your eyes are a bit bloodshot, are you ok?'

'Bit of a headcold. I'll be grand.'

'Okeydoke.'

We found the place. Pulled up in the big fancy car. There was a camera that makes a sound when you reverse. Just in case you hit anything. You know? Like things that are directly behind you. It started to beep and then we stopped. Dave pulled up the handbrake, said: 'Ok, which one is it?'

'That house over there. With the red car.'

He looked over. There was a group of mongs with hoods and tracksuits sitting on the wall.

'Looks dodgy.' Said Dave.

'They're just young lads.'

'Ok. I hope I don't get dog poo on my shoes.'

We got out. The mongs looked over. Assessed us. Muttered to themselves. Dave in the suit, stuck out fairly bad. The sun was dipping too and it was getting dark.

I remembered the place now. It was one of Jack's old areas. One of the first places he had brought me during the broadband job. And then I could see him. Out the top window. Watching events unfold. And it all came together. As I knew it would. Today was the day. The mongs started walking towards us.

Dave hesitated, said: 'John joe? Are you sure about this?'

## *They stole his shoes*

The robbery was swift and brutal. Jack had given me fair warning. I knew but I didn't know. He told me but he hadn't told me. Still, I didn't think I'd wake up in hospital. Bright light, smell of mash. Pain in my head. The doctor said: 'You're lucky.'

'Thanks. Did they get much?'

'You can ask the cops that.'

'Are they here?'

'Outside. I'll invite them in.'

They came in. Two plainclothes detectives. A tall fella with a Kerry accent. A woman from Galway. She said: 'Are you long working with this company, John joe?'

'About two months.'

'Anything like this ever happen before?'

'No.'

'Did you have any indication that you'd be robbed?'

'No.'

'Nobody told you?'

'No. Do they usually?'

'Do you know a *Jack Dalton*?'

'He got me the job.'

'He might also be the one responsible for the attack.'

'Jack? Why?'

'We've been keeping an eye on him lately.'

The fella stepped in, said: 'He's mixed up with some dangerous people.'

'Oh.'

'And we think he may have targeted you as an easy victim that would definitely have cash.'

'The bollix.'

The woman said: 'Have you seen him lately?'

'No.'

The fella said: 'We observed you recently talking in *The Shack.*'

'Oh yeah. Sorry. I'm confused with the head injury.'

'What were you talking about in *The Shack*?'

'His wife. How she went mad.'

'Anything else?'

'I can't remember.'

'About how much money do you think they got today?'

'I had collected €7000 and there was €7000 ready for doing the loans. So about €14000.'

'Are you sure about that?'

'That's all I had on me. Couldn't be anymore.'

'And there's none left at home or anything?'

'No.'

'Ok, we'll have to have your house searched too.'

'Why?'

'You might have been part of the robbery. If so, there might be cash there.'

'Sure I wasn't involved?'

'So you won't mind if we check?'

'Have I a choice?'

'Not really. It's a live investigation.'

They left. Fuck. Then Karen came in. Big tits, genuine concern, asked: 'Are you alright?'

'Yeah.'

'What were you doing?'

'Workin.'

'They robbed you because you sell Broadband?'

I told her the truth. She was ecstatic, said: 'Are you insane?'

'Maybe a little bit.'

'Debt collecting?'

'It's more Home Finance.'

'Don't be ridiculous.'

'What do you want me to say?'

'Jesus, John joe! What if my mother heard this?'

'Is that the point?'

'Or my father? Try telling *him* you're a Loan Shark!'

'Try telling him we needed the money.'

'Not *that* bad.'

'And it's *you* I'm marrying. Not your fuckin family. We can't all be fancy rich primary school teachers.'

'So you extort people instead?'

'There's no talkin to people like you.'

'People like who?'

'Fuckin snobs.'

'Lovely. I'll just put that down to your concussion.'

'Put it wherever you like.'

Beat. There was a family across the way feeling awkward. We let the rage calm. I asked: 'How's Dave?'

'Who's Dave?'

'My manager.'

'He's in intensive care.'

'Is he ok?'

'They stole his shoes.'

'Christ. What day is it?'

'Friday. Your stag is supposed to be tomorrow. You can't

go obviously.'

'Why not?'

'Because you're *here*.'

'Sure I'll be grand.'

'Grand? Great. Do what you like. I'll just cancel everything in the meantime, will I?'

And she stormed out.

Peace at last. My head was thumping. The sheets were awful tight. There was machines going in the next bed and some fella was snoring in the corner.

Karen had left a bottle of Diet 7up and Kimberley biscuits beside the bed. I tore them open, took three in my hand and wired into them. Then gulped down some 7up. Pure nutrition.

I looked at my phone. The group was still buzzing about the stag. Lads putting up pictures of pints and planes. As far as they knew, it was all still going ahead. Be an awful pity to disappoint them.

The doctor came back, white coat, smelled like carbolic soap, said: 'You need to rest.'

'I don't really. I need to go home.'

'Home? Ha. Not a hope.'

'Why not?'

'We need to do more tests.'

'How long will they take?'

'We'll do them this evening and keep you for the weekend for observation. Should have all the results by Monday and you'll be out by Tuesday.'

'I'm supposed to be goin to Spain tomorrow.'

'You can forget that.'

'It's my stag.'

'It could be your life if you don't stay here.'

'Are the guards gone?'

'Yes.'

'How's the man that was with me?'

'He'll pull through.'

And off he goes.

Would the guards find the money? Would I be connected to Jack? I could say I forgot about the €7000 if they found it. If they didn't, I'll keep it. Bring it to Madrid and drink it. My round lads. Speaking of drink, I could feel the shakes kicking in. I was still in my clothes. That helped. And there was an open window in the corner. That helped too. There was a drip on my arm. Fuck knows why. All I knew is it wasn't Grey Goose coming down the line and that didn't help at all.

So I said: 'Fuck this.'

I pulled out the drip and left through the window. The other patients were giving me funny looks but said nothing. Think they were too shocked, or thought they were imagining it.

Outside, there was a few bushes and grass and then I was in the carpark surrounded by the fresh air of freedom.

And there was a taxi rank across the road.

Beautiful.

## Back at the house

Back at the house. Karen said: 'What the hell are *you* doing here?!'

'They discharged me.'

'Really?'

'Sure I'm grand.'

'What about the tests?'

'They did them. Said there's nothin to worry about. Anything important, they'll ring me Monday.'

'So what now?'

'I've a flight in the morning.'

'Are you actually serious?'

'I can't let the lads down.'

'I don't want you sick for the wedding. The invites are gone out.'

'I'm not sick. I got a few slaps. Relax.'

'And you need to give up that ridiculous job. What would the other teachers say at work if they heard it?'

'They might ask me for a loan.'

'Cop yourself on.'

'You cop yourself on. It's not all about appearances either.'

'I don't want everyone thinking I'm marrying a thug.'

'Then don't marry me.'

'What are you talking about? It's all arranged.'

'So cancel it.'

'You're definitely concussed!'

'No point goin ahead if you're ashamed of me.'

'Excuse me?'

'We haven't been a couple for months.'

'Yes. And you know why. You couldn't possibly comprehend what I am going through.'

'You could try and explain? Or change the fuckin record.'

'Maybe if you were sober for ten minutes at a time.'

'We're dealin with it in different ways.'

'You can say that again.'

I looked around, asked: 'Were the guards here?'

'Yes.'

'Did they find anything?'

'They just looked around. They didn't take anything.'

'Nothin?'

'No. Why? What would they take? Have you got a stolen stack of televisions back there too? Or some pawn shop jewellery?'

'No. Just.'

'Go away.'

'Bitta bedside manner wouldn't go astray.'

'Just go to your stag and get it over with. I don't want to see you again for the rest of the weekend. I need time to process everything.'

I went and checked for the money. Took out the steel box and opened it up. Nothing budged. €7000 still there. Fuckin sound.

I peeled off two grand and put it in an envelope and left it there for the hotel. Then I thought about calling Jack but knew he'd be laying low for a few days. And the less contact the better. Wiser to go to Madrid and wait for it all to blow over.

Felt a sudden pain in my head, down the side of my neck, and in my chest. Remembered there was a naggin of Jim Beam in my locker. Found that and threw it back like a potent bourbon syrup of pain free dreams.

Problem solved.

## After the balaclavas

Meanwhile in London, after I turned on my phone and the crowd of headers burst through the window and took me away, I stopped thinking about home for a while.

They brought me off in a black van.

You know the van too. You've seen it, from the balcony, through the eyes of CCTV. How they came up fast with the masks and the batons, and then bundled me away.

I woke up a few hours later strapped to a chair. It was a dark room and I was surrounded by televisions. There was a room up ahead with a few weirdos in white coats looking at me through a glass wall. I could feel things stuck to my head, like the yokes they put on your chest when they're doing a heart exam. I tried to move but I was fairly tied down. And I was awful sore. I knew where this was going. *Clockwork Orange* stuff. I just didn't know *why.* That's when one of the scientists pressed a button and asked through the tannoy: 'Do you know why you're here, John joe?'

I shook my head in a way that said *No.*

I was too thirsty to shout. My answer seemed to confuse him because he looked at the clipboard and then turned to the others to discuss something. After, he hit the speaker again and went: 'Did nobody tell you?'

I shook my head again and he uttered a confused: 'Oh.'

They brought me to a large white room. The confused fella was sitting on a brown bingo chair and looking at his notes. He had a round face and black pants and red cheeks. When I sat down, he said: 'I'm Columba.'

'Howya, Columba.'

'I think we fucked up here.'

He was Irish. Galway accent. Great.

I went: 'Oh yeah?'

'Yeah. I don't think you should be here.'

'Where's *here*?'

'Do you not know?'

'No. Not a clue.'

'We'll go for a walk so, c'mon.'

He stood up and untied me and walked to the door. I followed him as best I could. I was a small bit crippled. We went by a water cooler, down a narrow corridor. Grey carpet. Tall high glass walled rooms to the left. Neon lights like a xenon hue. Columba in the white coat. An odd extra walking by, giving him the nod. There was a machinated hum somewhere, mechanical breathing, like huge fans or choleric engines.

Columba slowed up outside one of the glass rooms.

Inside, it had the bright blue, UV effect, two lads in hazmat suits with masks. There was an unconscious man strapped to a chair in the middle. Columba watched, ashen faced, said: 'This is test subject 2003.'

'What's he being tested for?'

'We think he's a candidate for quantum migration.'

'Is that a disease?'

'No.'

There was a big device at the back of the room. Donut dome effect surrounded by lights with a computer screen beside it. It looked like something for doing an MRI. The lads in the suits unhooked the fella being tested and lifted him over to the machine. Put him on the stretcher effort and rolled him into the dome.

They hooked up some wires to his body, chest and head; then closed the door so you couldn't see him anymore. After a few seconds there was a sound like scorched lightning and amplified wood burning. Columba shook his head and walked away.

Further on, there was more lads in science gear doing something with a swan. The swan kept squawking and spreading her wings and jumping around the place and they were trying to catch it and calm it down.

'I told them not to bring in that fuckin swan.' Said Columba. 'Swans are no good for experiments. Sure look at them? What data are they goin to get out of that? There'll be nothin but swan shit all over the fuckin floor.'

He knocked on the window. They didn't hear him. So he knocked harder, really rapped on it, said: 'Hey! Hey! Hey!'

One of the lab ducks looked over all concerned. Columba shouted: 'Take it out.'

'Where?' Asked the coat.

He pointed to the door, said: 'Back to where you found it.'

'What about the test?'

The swan sensed an opportunity here and attacked the other fella. Went for his leg with full anger and speed. The poor man jumped with fright and started screaming for help.

'Ah for fuck sake!' Said Columba. 'Get it out ta fuck!'

He turned to me, said: 'We better go for a pint. I'm dying for one.'

'Me too.'

'This place would break your fuckin heart.'

## *Be nice to the cow*

It was cold outside and hard to walk. We were on some street with buses and rain and *William Hill* betting shops. Everything was vibrant oxygen and roaring finance and rumbling history. It was hard to keep up with him but he didn't seem to mind. He whistled as he walked and rattled coins in his pockets and kept scanning the street for the nearest pub. When he found it he said: 'Ah.' And pushed in the door.

I hobbled in behind him. It was a quiet place, like an Indian restaurant, but it was really a bar. There was a weird looking fella in the corner wearing a red coat. He had a moustache and he kept smiling like a rat. I said: 'How's things?'

And he just nodded.

Columba asked: 'What're you havin?'

'Any kind of cider.'

'Orchard Thieves?'

'That'll do.'

He got the pints and we took a seat at a round table with a candle in the middle.

Could smell the candlewax, like a rural funeral. There was some kind of Mozart on the speakers. Soft violins. Piano Concertos. As good as *Lyric FM* around here. I took up the pint, cold glass, took a long swallow, sugar cane fields and clay and distant apples.

Columba said: 'Ok, so how did you get here?'

'On a plane.'

'I didn't mean literally. How did you end up at the institute?'

'I was kidnapped by a crowd of lads in balaclavas.'

'Had you turned on your phone?'

'I had.'

'See, that's where you went wrong.'

'How?'

'That's how they found you.'

'Do they just attack everyone that turns on phones?'

'Did you meet an old man?'

'I did. A pure dose.'

'That's him. A brother of mine.'

'He's your *brother*?'

'He is. God love him. Did he give you a letter?'

'Yeah.'

'And what did the letter say?'

'Twas all shite.'

He thought, looked around, asked: 'Are you hungry?'

'No.'

'I think I'll have a burger.'

'Do. Can I ask a few questions now?'

'Go on.'

'What's the story with the institute?'

He looked surprised, said: 'We're building the machine.'

'What machine?'

'What *machine?*'

'Jesus Christ.'

'No, not exactly.'

'I mean…Jesus Christ. What's going on?'

'I'm ordering a burger. Are you sure you don't want one?'

'Positive.'

The waiter came over. With the rodent teeth. Wrote the order down, looked to me, asked: 'And for you, sir?'

'Nothin. Thanks.'

His smile disappeared and he walked off.

Columba said: 'Nice place, this.'

'Can you explain a bit more about everything?'

'I thought you read the letter?'

'The first few pages.'

'And did you get to the bit about the machine?'

'Obviously not.'

'Oh.'

'What is it? What's the machine?'

'Pretty obvious, isn't it?'

'Not in the least.'

'Think about it. You're bound by the laws of physics in everything you do. Gravity, space-time, *time itself.* You believe that everything goes in one direction: Forward. Age, time, history. When a window breaks, it breaks into pieces - but why can't it reassemble itself again? We are locked into a system of rules which we need to break....'

'So you want to fix broken windows?'

'Imagine if we didn't need to obey the laws of creation – if we could ignore them and create our own? We could circumvent the creator, overcome the crisis, we'd all be like Nietzsche's Superman....except it wouldn't be just the mind, we could free the body too....'

'I'm lost. I haven't a fuck's clue what you're on about.'

'You met a girl called Cathy?'

'I did.'

'It was on your file.'

'So?'

'So you have potential for quantum migration. The first. We've been lookin for someone like you for years.'

'So that's why I'm in England?'

'Yes, it's why they brought you to the institute.'

'You said it was a mistake?'

'I did. I took you out for your own safety. They wanted to take apart your head.'

'Why?'

'Because you might hold the key to how it all works. They could even put you into the machine.'

'What happens if I go into the machine?'

'You saw it back there. You'll disintegrate into smithereens.' He took a drink, said: 'Cider's a bit dry, is it?'

'Tell me about the old man. Your brother.'

'Ludwig? He used to be in the Christian Brothers but was kicked out for being too serious.'

'That's an achievement. How'd he end up meeting Marilyn?'

'He was hangin around the place lookin for somethin to do. They were on to me at the institute to send him somewhere. Had all their hearts broke, tryin to get them to go sayin the Rosary. Shtop.'

'And?'

'And he heard about you and got all excited. Wanted to track you down so we let him go...we didn't think he'd actually succeed. Just wanted him to fuck off out of the way. He was looking for you in Athlone. Then followed you to Madrid and met Marilyn and she brought you here. She was supposed to bring you to the institute for human trials. Turns out it's not safe - as you no doubt observed. So I warned her about the danger and the plan had changed. But then you turned on your phone and ended up there anyway. I managed to convince them it *wasn't you* but they won't believe that for too long. You're the holy grail of the entire experiment. They're probably looking for us right now.'

'What does this have to do with Cathy?'

'The most crucial part of a quantum jump is to ensure

human consciousness can travel with the body so it can exist independently in a separate reality.'

'Is that what happened her?'

'We don't know. Maybe. That's all a bit weird.'

'Considering she killed herself.'

'Awful.'

'Was she here?'

'No. We don't know where she is. We picked up the ripple when you met her and it was the first time we had proof that this might be a realistic possibility. Up until then it was all theory and research. But now. Well.'

'Did you try and find her?'

'They tried. They went to her house, and then to her mother's old place and asked for you, and asked for her, but some undesirable called Derek kept demanding money so they had to leave again.'

The waiter came down. Left the burger on the table. There was chips beside it. I said: 'Can you bring two more pints aswell?'

'Certainly, sir. You killed the cow?'

'Heh?'

'The cow? You killed the cow.'

'Don't think so.'

Columba said: 'You used to work in an abattoir?'

'I did.'

'He's trying to say this burger contains meat from a cow you killed.'

I said: 'Oh.' Then: 'Any sign of them pints?'

Columba took a bite, spoke with a full mouth and said: 'Somehow you crossed over into a new reality with Cathy, and then back, and we don't know how. Did you ever see her again?'

'No.'

'Then tell me - how *did* you go from one physical realm

into the next and manage to return?'

'No idea. So what now?'

'I don't know. They're out of control here. Our reach is beyond our grasp and I don't want this to go any further. We're not far enough along for human testing. I should have never agreed to it. I've already handed in my notice.'

'And what are you going to do?'

'I'm applying for a taxi licence.'

'In England?'

'No. My mother is not well and I'm goin back to Galway. The money's not great here for taxis anyway. And I'll probably have to put Ludwig in a home somewhere.'

'So what do I do?'

'Let's have another pint and figure it out.'

'Who are *they*?'

'The people at the institute? They're an ugly bunch of fuckers. They want everythin done by last Tuesday.'

'And what was happening with the swan?'

'Oh fuck. Fuckin swans. Don't talk to me about swans. If I see one more fuckin swan.'

He took another bite, then asked: 'Were you generally happy when you killed the cows? I don't want to inherit any poor self-esteem.'

'I went to work singin every day. What do you think?'

'I think it's tasty nonetheless.'

'Fuck it, I might have one.'

'Least you could do.'

I looked around, got the waiter's attention. He came over. I said: 'I'll have a burger too there.'

'Just one burger?'

'Yeah.'

'Some chips for you?'

'Yeah, whatever he's havin.'

'Certainly, sir.'

'Weird lookin crayture.' Said Columba.

'He'll be dead in three years.'

'How?'

'Drug resistant TB.'

'Christ above. At least you know you have second sight.'

'What's that mean?'

'Knowin things like that.'

'Like what?'

'Knowing he'll be dead in three years. It's a glimpse, a quantum algorithm. Society call it madness, schizophrenia. Jesus had it and look how that worked out.'

'So they'll be crucifying me next?'

'Worse, if the crowd at the institute don't get you, you'll be locked up by people that think you're crazy. They'll dry out your mind. Kill your spirit with drugs and new age psychology. Brainwash you into believing it's all in your head and say you have no gift. They'll do everything they can to wipe out the truth because it's too hard to understand. It's too dangerous. It means everything we believed up to now is wrong. Think about Copernicus, Galileo...'

'I'm lost again.'

'Just be careful what you tell them if you wake up.'

'Wake up?'

'From the coma.'

'What coma?'

He looked at me, pure owl eyes, said: 'You're in a coma in Athlone.'

I thought: *Aragh fuck this,* said: 'Is that right?'

'After you got attacked. You split. You're *here.* And you're *there.* This is why we wanted you so bad. You're in a pure state of flux, a perfect specimen.'

'Great to be a specimen.'

'I'd imagine so.'

Two pints and he's talking pure shite. I tried to think of more questions, just for the sheer torture of it. The best I could manage was: 'What's a quantum jump?'

'It's like going and coming back before anyone knows you're gone.'

'What's so great about that?'

'Imagine a room full of mirrors with multiple reflections...'

'Yeah...'

'And each reflection is a different reality.'

'Ok.'

'And imagine there's already a version, or mirror image, of everyone that got hit by a bus, died from disease, fell off a mountain, crashed a car, got married, shot, fell in love, had kids, it doesn't matter - everything has already happened and the reality we experience is that particular version instead of any of the others....imagine you could jump to the version where you didn't crash the car, or fall off the mountain, or whatever it might be...and that's what happened with Cathy....she was alive. You jumped from one mirror to the next and back....'

'Doesn't sound that bad.'

'You're missing the point. As humans, we think we have a choice. We're arrogant enough to believe that everything is because we chose it to be so...but it's not. There's an underlying pattern. A system of mathematical infinity that we could never possibly understand. This is like a man trying to do brain surgery on himself.... we're pulling at the seams of existence and I'm not confident we can handle it as a species.'

'So why are they doin it?'

'Money. Why else?'

'Money?'

'Horse racing, stock market, football games. It can all be manipulated. Imagine, you could jump over to the version of yourself that picked the right horse, then jump back.'

'Still doesn't sound that bad.'

'Until the horse wins.'

'Why?'

'Because then you have two realities with the same outcome and both mirrors will smash. Both versions will compete for the same time and space and there'll be astronomical pressure – enough to tear open a hole in *space-time* and swallow us into infinite nothing. The opposite of the big bang. We'll all quietly evaporate like a liquid bubble bursting in the silent bleakness above....'

'I still don't see how I can help.'

'They want to take apart your brain. They won't ask your permission.'

'Will they not listen to *you*?'

'Not anymore. They needed me to get to this point. I'm a world expert on quantum worlds but I never wanted to do anything unethical. I wanted to prove the science. I wanted a breakthrough for the sake of humanity but it turns out this other crowd want to rig the fuckin lotto. It didn't really matter until you turned up, but now it's a different story...'

Silence. The poor man was definitely cracked. I was dying for a piss, said: 'I'll be back in a minute.'

'Ok. Just don't let them cure you.'

'Who?'

'You'll know soon enough.'

The back of the pub was dark and it was awkward to find

the toilets.

Eventually I found the door, lit up by the flash of a poker machine. Walked in. Dead silent. Bright walls. A smell like lavender. Thought about what next. That cider was going down well, like the hint of a good session. Had a piss. Washed my hands. Wondered what shite Columba would be talking next. I might need a vodka to take the edge off.

When I came back he was gone. I looked around. Couldn't see him anywhere. I gave it a few minutes, but no sign. My burger had arrived too and I was starved so I picked it up and took a huge bite. I didn't remember killing it but it was damn nice.

I took another few bites. Had a few chips. Washed it all down with the Orchard Thieves. After a while, I had to go. Sure, I was just sitting there on my own like a tool.

The fella with the red suit was at the door on my way out. He held it back for me, said: 'Good night, sir.'

'Good night.' I said.

'You will have a good evening?'

'I hope so.'

'Be nice to the cow'

'I will.'

'You will.'

## *The Queen's face*

Somewhere in the ether, the first notes of *Karma Police, Radiohead*. Might have been a passing car, a passing phone, a loner whistling in the night. I let the worm take hold, soothe the chemicals across the moon of my fuzzy thoughts. It was like some kind of sad hope or dying despair. And the streets were busy with cars and drunk wankers in skinny jeans and fat women in loud shoes. There were trains overhead and sirens in the distance and a smell like rubber coming up from the vents. I saw a big red and white sign that pointed to the underground so I went there. Down steps that had a whiff of piss and through a long white corridor with huge advertisements either side. There was a West End Musical. An ad for aftershave. Someone had made a production out of George Orwell's *1984*. My father used to talk about the book. Something about cameras.

I walked to the platform. That smell of dead hot air and mechanised souls. The haunting hangover of progress towards stagnation. Everyone going somewhere different, feeling like they're on the wrong train, like there's a faster train to somewhere else they should be. A different direction. Another track. A promise of soon. They rushed by, and talked on phones, and smelled like wine. There were groups and loners and beggars and lonely women and scared women and indifferent men and people coming from work and going to work. There was a big rush of wind and then a train came that had *Piccadilly Circus* written on the top. It halted with a screech and the doors flew open and people puked out and scattered and then everyone else rushed on, and did crosswords, and read books and listened to headphones and lived between the stations. I hung on to the yoke to stop you falling and read the map on the wall. Didn't matter what it said because it was all the same to me but I wanted to look like I was doing something. Like I had a purpose. You wouldn't know who'd be looking. I thought about a plan. Things were getting scrappy. Lads trying to use my brain to break the bookies. I wasn't a fan. And where did Columba go? Prick could have said goodbye.

I got off in Leicester Square. Now we're talking. First place I saw was a Casino. I checked my wallet and found Karen's credit card. Hopefully she hadn't cancelled it yet. I went to the ATM in the corner. Withdrew £500. The machine purred and gave it to me. I fuckin love it. Was never so happy see the Queen's face.

My first stop was Roulette. I put the £500 on Black and lost it. I felt sad and vindicated at the same time. Then I remembered what Columba was saying about the predictions. According to him I should be a psychic Paddy and be able to clean the place out. I hit the card for another £500. Got it. Put it all on Red and won. Now I was even. Green Zero was calling me. 36-1. How're ya fixed?

Decided to postpone the riches for a while until I played some poker. Walked over. Took a seat. Green felt. Airborne dopamine. Nodded to the dealer. He was black, in a waistcoat, no big smile. Efficient with the cards. He dealt me in. Two cards and a stack of chips and fuck the world after that.

There was a lot of clowns around the table. One fella wearing sunglasses, another kept talking shite like it was a tactic. Everyone thinking they were on *PokerStars*. I started winning money. The cards were going my way. Your man that kept talking eventually focused on me.

'What have you got there, John joe?' He asked.

I had two Kings, went: 'How'd you know my name?'

'I guessed. You look like a John joe. Irish, huh?'

'Yeah, what's wrong with that?'

'You all have bad teeth, right?'

'What the fuck's that got to do with anythin?'

'It's like, somebody give those guys a couple of toothbrushes or somethin…'

'You a dentist?'

He laughed, complimented, went: 'No, I'm in Real Estate.'

'Property like? You sell houses?'

'That's my bread and butter.'

'Do you need teeth for that?'

He smiled, a big white set of perfect chompers, said: 'Of course.'

'You better shut the fuck up so or I'll knock out every one of them with a shlap.'

'Say what, fella?'

'Play your cards and stop talking shite.'

There was two Jacks on the board. Giving me two pair. Kings High.

Real Estate hadn't said anything for a few seconds, which was an eternity by his standards. Then he went: 'Ok, Paddy big mouth, let's put you all in.'

'All in?'

'All in.'

I had about £8000 by now. Enough to keep me going for a good while. How was I winning? I didn't know. Just had an instinct of when to bet and when to fold. *Rain Man* here. Then again, I'd have nothing at all if I lost this hand. But sure I was quantum leap. Invincible. Real Estate thought he was Phil Ivy, keeping it cool. I said: 'Sound, so. Call.'

And he twitched like his bowels were after melting and there was scutter going down his leg.

'Turn them.' I said.

He turned over a pair of tens. Riding on the Jacks high. I flipped my Kings and there was a sigh around the table.

'Sorry about that.' I said, as insincere as I could manage.

'Fuck you.' He said.

'Gracious in defeat. Good man.'

'Asshole.'

'Stick to the Real Estate now, good lad.'

'Fuckin Irish.'

'I'll buy you a pint out of my winnings if you promise to shut up for the next hand.'

'I don't want your charity.'

'You might need it though.'

'Tuh.'

That's when I saw the cops coming in the door. There was a good chance they were looking for *me*. Just had that feeling. Maybe the credit card had me twigged somewhere. I pulled all the chips together, quietly cashed them and went out the back door.

## *Rough draft of a cliched God*

Outside. Alleyway. Evening. Dusk. The first lad I saw was Ludwig, the old man, bent over like pilates gone wrong, rough draft of a cliched God, like he'd been waiting for me. I don't know why, but I was terrified for a second. He asked: 'Did you read the letter?'

I hadn't time so I kept going. Walked fast up an alley of dirty puddles and bins and old drink crates. I shouted back: 'Gimme a shout later. I'll tell you what I think.'

I was waiting for him to say something but when I turned around he was gone. Sure isn't that more of it now? The cops burst through the door then.

*Miami Vice* job.

They looked left, then right, then saw me.

'Hey, you!' Said one of them in an English accent. 'Stay where you are.'

But I was already running. I got around the corner. Ran by some theatres and pizza places. Wouldn't mind a slice of Pepperoni but said I better not.

Then Marilyn pulled up in the car and guess what she said?

So I got in.

'You're a fool.' She said.

'I am, I suppose.'

'I found the letter torn up on the ground.'

'It bored me to tears.'

'Lucky he didn't see it.'

'Speakin of luck. I won fifteen grand.'

'Was it luck or premonition?'

'Bit of both I think.'

'Good. You're finally getting it.'

'You think I can crack the lotto too?'

'I know you can.'

'And himself was back there too?'

'Who?'

'The prick that gave me the letter. Pope Pius…'

'He was?'

'Yeah, outside the Casino.'

'Ok, we need to go back to the flat and wait.'

'Did you see your windows?'

'Yes. I told you not to plug in your phone.'

'They brought me to an institute.'

'It's where they bring everybody. Did you meet Columba?'

'I did. And then he disappeared on me.'

'Ok. We should just wait for Ludwig.'

'Who? The 90-degree angle?'

'Yes. He'll know how to proceed.'

'Oh great. More waitin for Ludwig so. He sounds like a species of beetle.'

'You should be honoured he's taking the time to talk to you.'

'I am. Honestly. Look at me. I'm overwhelmed.'

Back at her place. There was a smell like spilled cider and cold wind. The glass had been cleaned up but the curtains flew in the air like a bad ghost.

I took a seat on the couch. Marilyn's heels clicked on the wood floor. She opened the fridge. Took out a bottle of beer, opened it and drank. Then she walked over and gave it to me and went into the bedroom.

It was quiet so I put on the telly. There was news reports

about starvation, war and volcanoes erupting. All great news in general. I sipped the beer and hoped things would start making sense. They didn't. I thought about home. Wondered if Fidelma the photographer was still waiting for the money in her account. Karen had probably burned everything belong to me by now. Marilyn walked in, asked: 'So I take it you're not getting married anymore?'

'Highly unlikely.'

'Lucky girl. Dodged a landmine with you.'

'Jez, calm down with the compliments there.'

'This is your chance to start something new.'

'Like a relationship? With you?'

'A new direction in life. Look outside.'

'Am I stayin here so?'

'We'll see what he says.'

'Mr. Neck? Great. I feel I'm in a weird dream.'

'Most people never wake up their whole lives. Look around. You're in London. One of the most incredible cities in the world. Endless possibility. Can't you feel that exciting breeze?'

'It's from the broken window. And I'm hungry.'

'What would you like?'

'Pizza.'

'I'll order it.'

'Good.'

## Let the burn sing and dance

The pizza came in a large square box and smelled like melted cheese and dripping meat. I bit hard and it burnt my mouth and lips and I said: 'Fuck!'

'Wait til it cools down.' Said Marilyn.

'Bit late tellin me now.'

I sat back on the couch. Let the burn sing and dance. There was a copshow on the telly. Some two lads talking about a case going wrong. I took another beer out of the fridge. Drank it. Thought about ale and hops, and plants, and farmers in far off fields. Sunburnt straw hats and the quiet unpolluted distance. Then a machine somewhere, and steam, and wheels and cogs like from inside a big watch.

Marilyn asked: 'So how much did Columba tell you?'

'Somethin about takin out my brain?'

'Did he mention you're in a coma?'

'He did. I thought he was raving.'

'You're on a different level. A different version of yourself.'

'Yeah, a pure specimen he called me.'

'Yes. Somehow you have two simultaneous existing realities. That's the key to everything. Tell me about the debt collecting. And Cathy.'

'How did you know about the debt collecting?'

'It's all part of it. You. That. Cathy. You're the first two people in history from different realities to sleep together.'

'Do we win somethin for that?'

'It's what makes it real. The physical contact. The theory is consummated.'

'So we're married? By a theory?'

'It's a proven theory now. It's a new principle of physics.'

Her phone rang. She looked at it, said: 'It's him. Hang on.'

She took the call in the bedroom. Left me on my own with the pizza.

Ten minutes later, she came back, said: 'Ludwig's not coming.'

'Why not? I was looking forward to seeing him. Sure he's great craic.'

'He thinks he's being followed and says it's too dangerous.'

'What's the big plan so?'

'We have to go back to Ireland.'

'Why?'

'If they can't find *you*, they're going straight to the source – the hospital.'

'And what'll happen when they get there?'

'They'll take your body and bring it back to the institute and experiment.'

'So what do we do?'

'We plug you out.'

'How's that work?'

'It'll close the loop. Back to one singular reality.'

'And what happens to me then?'

'Theoretically nothing. That universe collapses and you go on as normal in this one.'

'Normal?'

'Anyway, you'll feel the effects of whatever they do if they take you – like a Voodoo doll. And I'm sure you don't want *that*? So we're flying back to Athlone tomorrow.'

'It doesn't have an airport.'

'Ok, Dublin then and we'll rent a car. Is the hospital in the town?'

'Yeah. And I have a Vectra.'

'What's that?'

'My car.'

'It sounds like something from Star Wars.'

'You don't know the half of it.'

'We'll go straight from the airport in your space machine then.'

'Mighty.'

'And the pizza is cold now.'

I took a slice. She was right but my taste buds were already fucked so it didn't matter.

Later, we made love. Intimate and surreal. I kissed every part of her body, tasted her entire soul. She was light on top of me, deft. Entering her was a thing of invited invasion. She gasped a little, in a way that persuaded me to push harder. We rolled around the black sheets, let the air caress our sweaty backs and her moist hair. She had a vibrator and asked me to use it on her. Then she took it herself and told me to get hard while she got there. Later, she slept on my stomach, her hand touching my face and her finger touching my lip. I could taste it, the metallic taste of perfumed woman. Everything was calm after passion as the dawn crept softly through the window. For a second I forgot. Everything was perfect. Then I remembered. Back to Ireland tomorrow. Fuck.

## Back in Dublin

On the plane. All pine needles of nostalgia for the night before. Marilyn was fluid, water beauty, swimming through the grime untarnished. Shine from her auburn hair, black leather pants, heels. That perfume that turns heads toward forgotten dreams. We sat down. They gave us newspapers. It was a short flight but fuck it. Read it anyway. There was politics, sport, and a piece about a murderous feud in Athlone. Two dead already. A hunt on for a suspect. Known to the guards. Couldn't be named for legal reasons. Was possibly on the run. Then we landed. Tarmac. Pissed off Dublin people. Spaniards looking up *Temple Bar* on their phones. My throat dry from the circulated air. Being back felt like a relapse, the end of remission.

Marilyn asked: 'Where are you parked?'

'It's not far.'

We walked through the terminal. Her with the sunglasses. Rock stars.

Escalators. Got out on to the departures and there was a mystic breeze, like diesel ghosts. Into the car park. Eyes adjust, world dims. The sun was autumnal, low, calm. Golden shafts across the concrete floor.

There was the Vectra waiting, like a patient dog.

We sat in. Started her up. A strong purr. *Lyric FM* were straight in with *The Funeral March*. I felt ok with Marilyn beside me. Powerful, dangerous, indestructible.

Asked her: 'So where do we go now?'

'Straight to the hospital.'

'How do you think I'll feel when I plug myself out?'

'I don't know.'

'Doesn't sound that scientific really.'

'Let's just go with Ludwig's advice for the moment.'

'Fuckin great.'

We took off. Signs for Belfast, Cavan, Cork, Waterford, Limerick. Eventually saw the exit for Galway and The West. Took that. Road flows underneath the car. And the car eats up the road. And the wind comes strong and the rain falls like an old friend. We got to Athlone like a comet in a hurry. Took the Coosan exit and went up by Clonbrusk.

Came in by Assumption Road and took a left into St. Vincent's. We pulled up in the car park. It was fairly empty. The sun was gone down and it was pure dark. We got out and walked over to the door. There was a smell like sweet smoke and exhaust fumes. Lame drizzle from the damp leaking sky.

The doors opened automatically. We walked in. Smell of disinfectant. Went down the corridor. It was quiet and people didn't take much notice of us. Marilyn went up to the desk and asked them where to find me. The receptionist looked up the computer and told her.

After, we went there. Through a door, through a red fog of the mind. Felt like I was going through a musty room, with old furniture, and worn chairs, and rattling windows, and gaudy stained golden cutlery. I could hear the silence of the thick walls and see the paintings. Old portraits of generations of people I had never known, but always known, and couldn't remember. Some other life, other place, other time. A sky like a bowl of blue water. And then.

Seeing yourself in a coma is strange. You're there on the bed with the tubes and the whole lot and you're looking at yourself at the same time. Stranger still was the two detectives. The one with the Kerry accent and the woman from Galway. The Kerryman looked up, assumed recognition, asked: 'Can I help you?'

## *The €7000*

I looked around and Marilyn was gone. Could just see the back of her head going under a bush outside. Sneaky bitch. Now the handcuffs were out. They wanted to arrest me over the €7000 I had held back from the robbery.

I pointed to the bed and tried to tell them I was in a coma. But they said it wasn't me. That was my boss *Dave*. And how the hell could I be in a coma and talking to them at the same time? And why would I want to plug out the poor man's oxygen?

Then they led me away. Brought me down to the station. We pulled up outside. People were looking at uswhile they smoked at the door of The Bailey across the road. There was the sound of bells from the church by the bridge. It was cold too, brazen wind. Inside, there was people signing the attendance book. Posters on the wall about Anti-Social Behaviour. A smell like crayons and orange peels. They asked if I wanted to make a phone call but I couldn't think of anyone. Marilyn maybe, but she had some gammy English number and I didn't know it. I could try Karen but what would I say? After that. Well. There was nobody else. So they took some details and brought me to an interview room.

It was more of a stuffy square box down the back. The guard with the Kerry accent was called Pat. He had blue eyes and a tight hair cut. Arrogant air, like the vet I hit with the sheep's liver that time. Mags was more relaxed. Had the look of a woman partial to a spicebag and twenty fags. Took her lead from Pat.

There was two plastic bags on the table. Something looked familiar, recognizable. I leaned in and looked closer. Black handles, silver blades. They asked me a few questions about Anthony, Jack's boss, the fella with the poker machines. And did I know his girlfriend? Rachel?

And was I aware Jack was sleeping with her?

Then they decided to explain a few things. Someone had

cut out Rachel's heart and fed it to Jack. Then someone had cut off Jack's testicles and stuffed them down Rachel's throat. It was the double murder they'd been talking about in the paper. An expert job, done by someone with experience, say, someone that might have worked in a slaughterhouse one time and was familiar with cutting up animals. Someone fairly good with knives.

All in all, I'd missed a fair bit of drama. I asked if they'd talked to Anthony. They said they had.

And?

No evidence. No leads. But they weren't interested in him anymore. They had a new theory.

What's that?

They knew I had stolen money because they'd arrested one of the mongs that attacked me and he swore blind they'd only gotten €7000. And they checked with the office and knew I should have €14000. And there's anecdotal evidence of John joe buying for the house in Spain and helping himself to prostitutes. And what's this few thousand sterling doing in your back pocket? Poker is it? You must have been robbing for a long time, were ya?

The way they were going to spin it was I had attacked Jack over the robbery and killed him. And Rachel was there too so she had to go because she was a witness. And then I had cut out their hearts and testicles and all that and went on the run to London. And sure it all made sense. We have your knives here, from the slaughterhouse, and we're going to send them to forensics. Check for DNA, fingerprints, all that fancy crime drama stuff.

And what about me blaming Conal for the bombscare at the airport? They put all that together now too. And stealing Karen's credit card? They even had Fidelma, the wedding photographer, saying I was a liar and prone to scams. The fuckin bitch had called the cops. And why were you harassing your customers saying you were going to rape their dead relatives? And there you were this evening trying to plug out poor Dave. Trying to cover your tracks, were ya? He must have been on to you, was he? A real crime spree here, John joe. Can we have a statement please? Maybe get *your side* of this strange story.

I asked: 'Where do I start?'

Kerry Pat said: 'Let's talk about when you got attacked at Oakpark, before you left for Madrid. We're fairly sure of everything up until then.'

Mags took out some sheets and a biro. Scribbled a bit on the top of the page to see if it was working. Then she looked up and said: 'Would you like a cup of water?'

'Any chance of a vodka?'

'No.' Said Pat. 'Start talking.'

So I started talking. Took about an hour. There was an awkward silence after.

Between all the talk about different realities, mental sex and quantum jumps and gambling scams they reckoned I was stone mad altogehter. Figure that.

## *Amanda*

I was put in a place for the criminally insane. Cuckoo's nest job. Tablets. Headcases. Lads in straitjackets. Spent a good month there. The cell was like a big square white box with a bed. Most of the time was wanking and thinking about Marilyn. But even that got old after a while. I couldn't understand why she hadn't made contact yet. I was starting to forget her. What she looked like, how she felt in my arms. It was a phantom memory, fading away as the days went by. The food was pure muck too. Hard peas and dodgy mash with tangy chicken and a cup of milk. They couldn't even give me right knives and forks in case I stabbed the staff, or another patient, or myself. Had to use the white plastic yokes. Dose.

Then one morning there was a knock on the door. The nurse said I had a visitor. Maybe it was Marilyn? All the love and hope flooded back. A solution, an explanation, the chance of escape. So I walked out, cocky, confident, ready to smile and be free. But it wasn't her. It was a lady in a short skirt and a black jacket. Golden hair. Big blue eyes. Fake tan. Red painted nails. Some kind of badge or lanyard with her picture on it. She looked fatter on the image, bloated, full of water. She had a folder with a drawing of a smiling sun on the front.

She said: 'Hello, John joe.'
Smoker's husk. Broken vocals.
I said: 'Hello.'
'My name is Amanda.'
'Howya, Amanda.'
'I'm here for your mental health evaluation.'
'Ah, right. How's that work?'
'We talk. I make some assessments. And write a report.'
'Why?'
'We need to keep an eye on you and make sure your mind doesn't deteriorate.'

'What about the version of me that's in the coma?'
'That's the kind of thing we're talking about.'
'How do you mean?'
'How can you think you're in a coma and be *here* at the same time?'
'Cos I am. I saw myself.'
'But that's impossible.'
'And sure here we are.'
'You have been having delusions.'
'Like I'm imagining things?'
'Yes. It's possibly a schizoid disorder.'
'How did I get that?'
'It's a disease of the mind. There's no exact cause. Do you have issues at the moment?'
'No. I never had.'
'I'm afraid to say that you exhibit certain behaviours that would appear....worrying.'
'Like cutting out people's hearts and testicles?'
'That included, yes.'
'But that wasn't me.'
'It might have been a fragmented version of you.'
'Eh....no. Unless the fragment is called Anthony and we're the same person.'
'There's no evidence to suggest anyone else was responsible.'
'No evidence against me either.'
'We're still waiting on the knives.'
'Be some craic when they come back negative. When did I even do it?'
She looked through the folder, found a page, said: 'It was before you went to London. Remember the police came looking for you in *The Shack*?'
'Yeah.'
'You had a fight with Karen. You say she knocked you unconscious after you told her about sleeping with a prostitute in Madrid?'

'Ok.'

'We think that was the black out. When it happened.'

'So I just went and found Jack and Rachel and decided to kill them?'

'Yes.'

'And there's no real evidence?'

'Not yet. But the optics aren't good. Surely you can understand? You were in a conspiracy to steal money. He double crosses you. You end up in hospital. You come back from Madrid and go to confront him and it gets out of hand....'

'Except I didn't do it.'

'Or you don't remember.'

'And there was no conspiracy.'

'But you ended up with serious injuries after the robbery?'

'I don't think they meant to hurt us that bad.'

'But still, you wanted revenge?'

'No.'

'Well some part of you obviously did. He was supposed to be the Best Man at your wedding and he treats you like that?'

'You're reading it all wrong. And I never even met Rachel.'

'Never?'

'Never. And I didn't go on the run. I went to meet Marilyn. You need to find her. She came with me from London.'

'I'm afraid there was *nobody* with you.'

'Ask the guards. Pat and Mags. They can look up the CCTV in the hospital and see me walking in with her.'

'They did. They claim you were alone.'

'And what was I doing there?'

'At the hospital?'

'Yeah, why was I there? Why were *they* there?'

'They were about to interview your manager *Dave* before you came and tried to plug out his oxygen....'

'I was trying to plug myself out.'

She sighed, said: 'Let's talk about this idea of two realities.'

'I thought they don't exist according to you?'

'I want to get a sense of how certain you are and maybe we can poke some holes in the logic and make you see it's a delusion.'

'Ok.'

'When do you think you first had symptoms?'

I told her about Cathy. The voices. A few other bits and pieces.

She said: 'And you had no way of knowing this Cathy girl before?'

'Sure how could I?'

'Even from years ago? Any connection at all?'

'No.'

'You're *sure* about that?'

'Certain.'

'Tell me more about Jack.'

I told her all I knew about Jack. And Anthony, and the whole lot. Then we got on to England.

After, she said: 'Ok. we have a lot to work through here.'

'Who are ya tellin? They warned me about you.'

'Who?'

'Columba. He told me you'd come and try to brainwash me.'

'Do you believe that?'

'He said: *"Don't let them cure you."*'

'I can't help you if you refuse to admit you have a problem.'

'Convince me.'

'I'll be back next week.'

'I'm innocent. You need to get me out of here.'

'I can help you with your mental illness but I can't work miracles. The public are screaming for a win against crime. And, let's be honest, right now – you're the best thing on offer.'

## *Damien*

There was big talk about a trial. I was given a solicitor through free legal aid. His name was Damien. A young lad in a creased suit. Cheap phone and a battered watch.

He came to visit me twice a week. His skin was all red and blotched, like he was after getting stung by nettles or poison ivy. Always had the look of being eternally embarrassed. He even had a black folder but there didn't seem to be much in it. Just a notepad and a biro and an old calculator. Like what they give you when you start a sales job.

He said I had a case. Insanity. Distress. Madness. I said how about *innocence?* Would that work? And he smiled an awkward smile. Then I asked him how he got here and he said he got the bus. Sure that was enough.

I kept hoping Marilyn might turn up with a plan. Some kind of breakout scheme. But no sign of her. Damien kept me up to date on the case and the perception on the outside. He usually stole the free paper from *Supermacs* and we'd read it. It was a big media event. Biggest in a long time. They were calling me *Just eat John joe.* Quotes from Karen disowning me.

And her father saying he always thought I was a bit *off*.

Wrong.

Strange.

And Derek had rang the tabloids with my story about sleeping with Cathy so there was another headline calling me the *Shylock Sex Pest*.

Damien still reckoned my defence was strong. He was a bit thin on detail, but said he was working on it. There was other cases like mine before where the lads had got away with it. I asked him who and he couldn't think of their names, just said he read about them on the internet. But he'll print it out and bring it in the next time.

I told him thanks, you're mighty. When's the case, I asked

him.

Not sure, he said. I'll look into it. The prosecution are hoping for more evidence first. No forensics back yet. Then he had to go because he was afraid he might miss the bus.

When I wasn't talking to Damien I was in the cell. At night, it was dark and cold. The walls austere. The bed hard. Like being in a glass bowl but the glass was made of concrete. A bright thick sheen on the walls. Bars on the windows. Terrible silence.

I replayed everything in my head. Maybe I *was* truly mad?

Some nights I'd dream it all again but this time it would be different. I'd just marry Karen and we'd have a house somewhere and we'd be normal. No funerals. No Marilyn. Cathy. Quantum shite. And Rachel and Jack would still be alive.

And then I'd wake up.

And it would be worse. I would be terrified. Proper shaking with my teeth clattering. I'd call out to the nurses but they paid no heed. Just another nutjob killer facing his demons, feeling the karma.

Other nights I wouldn't be able to sleep at all and I'd lie there looking at the ceiling. I would sense something at the end of the bed. Some presence. Some force. A light. A warmth. A glow. I'd look up and Rachel would be standing there. Overweight. Blonde hair, tattoos, blue eyes. Her throat and chest all cut and her face white and gaunt. And she'd be there looking at me, wearing her nightgown, and her hair would be tossed and her eyes bloodshot.

The first night I tried to talk to her. Tried to say something. But she wouldn't talk back. I said: 'Rachel. I'm sorry. It wasn't me.'

Another night I saw Jack there too. He was sitting on a chair. Denim jacket, brown shoes. His chin up like a Leprechaun. Smoking rollies. He just sat there and laughed. A loud echo, full with sarcasm. I can still hear it. The way it bounces off the walls of my head. Of the cell. Of my mind.

## Leaflets about AIDS

The meetings with Amanda became a weekly thing. Going through everything. Unearthing incidents. My childhood. My past. Did I enjoy killing the animals in the abattoir? Who trained me? How long did I work there? Why was I fired? Did I ever engage in bestiality?

What was the intimacy like with Karen?
Anything unusual? Bondage? Sado-masochism?
Did I have any brothers and sisters?
Who was the first girl I slept with? And when?
Did I ever use prostitutes that weren't imaginary?
Had I ever participated in proper necrophilia?
Did I enjoy violent films? Did I ever get aroused by them?

They had us in a private room now for the sessions. Said it was a better ambience for therapy. I wasn't sure. Bland enough set up. Bored plant in the corner. Coffee table with leaflets about AIDS. Cameras on in case I attacked her.

One day I asked: 'What about *you*?'
She crossed her legs, said: 'What about me?'
She was in tights today, and a red leather skirt and red shoes. Busty black top.
'What are *you* into?'
'I'm not the patient here.'
'You must think about it though?'
'About what?'
'Every time you sleep with someone: Is he crazy? Why does he like that? What makes him want that? Blah blah blah….'
'Some things are indicators. Others are quirks.'
'So what do I have?'
'Indicators.'
'Says who?'
'Says the research.'
'What research? I'm not goin around flashing people.'

'Do you accept that Marilyn never existed?'
'How could I?'
'Did you ever see her in the company of another person?'
'Ludwig.'
'You mean the old man that gave you a letter?'
'Him, yeah.'
'Do you see a connection here? Between the two illusions combining?'
'I slept with her. In Madrid.'
'I'm sure you believe that.'
'Because it happened. And in London too.'
'Nobody flew with you on the flight back. There was nothing on CCTV from the airport or anywhere all the way to Athlone. There was nobody there.'
'I told Karen about her.'
'Did she meet her?'
'No. But she heard the call when...'
'What call?'
'I got a call from Spain when I got back.'
'Yes, you forgot to pay for the hotel.'
'What?'
'You left and didn't pay. That's why they were calling you...from Spain....'
'Jack booked it. I thought he had it sorted. He was supposed to collect money from everyone and I wouldn't have to pay because it was my stag....'
'Obviously not. That's the call Karen heard and assumed it was something to do with a lady you met. And then you admitted it...the second call to come to London was imaginary.'
Beat.
Then I asked: 'Christ...what about Columba then?'
'The man from the institute you mentioned?'
'Yeah.'
'Doesn't exist. There's nobody called Columba on any scientific records from Galway or London. No institute like you described. Nothing.'

'So what *did* I do in London?'

'You got drunk a lot, and went to a Casino, and the rest is part of a psychotic break.'

'Or the rest is when everythin else happened.'

'I know you *feel* it's real. I know you *believe* it's real. And it's identical to *reality* in your mind. But….it *didn't* happen. You were mentally ill and didn't know. The tragedy of the miscarriage, the toxic relationship, and the pressure of getting married, tipped you over the edge and your brain created an illusory world to help you cope.'

'Or maybe it's true?'

Tested patience, she spoke again: 'There were signs all along. You just didn't see them. Like I said: Indicators.'

'It still doesn't explain the thing with Cathy.'

She cleared her throat, looked at her notes. Her hair was loosely tied, black tinge coming through the roots.

She found what she was looking for, said: 'The police checked the system at your office. Nobody with her name borrowed any money.'

'Then where did it go?'

'You probably spent it on alcohol. They talked to Yvette. There *was* an imbalance that particular week and the risk officer was preparing an investigation.'

'Then who called me to do the loan?'

'Derek.'

'Who?'

'Derek. The man that lives with Cathy's sister. He used Mary's old phone because he had no credit and he called you and asked you for a loan and you turned him down. Then you arrived at the house.'

'Jesus.'

'That's how Mary's number was on your phone. How you called her back and why he denied it – in case you refused him again. Do you remember? He told you he'd break your face with a brick? He confessed all this to the investigators.'

'How could I have known about Cathy?'

'You said it yourself. You talked to dozens of people every day. Telling you their problems, stories, life events. You heard their voices at night. You heard about Cathy from somebody, repressed it, then it manifested in your delusion.'

I was dizzy, scared, like the anchor on my sanity was after lifting, said: 'Now I'm really fucked up.'

'It's hard to hear but it's a breakthrough. We now have two competing realities and can categorically prove *one* and *disprove* the other.'

'How is this possible?'

She was sympathetic, genuinely sad for me, said: 'You're sick, John joe, that's all it is. Don't worry, we'll get there.'

I thought of Karen. Her lying on my chest, crying after that day in the hospital. Before she decided it was all my fault.

Then I asked: 'Does anyone even *suspect* Rachel's partner, Anthony, who is already known as a psychotic killer?'

'Of course. But he's been exonerated. The case against you is more compelling.'

'How so? There's still no evidence.'

She paused, then said: 'I'm afraid there is.'

'Like what?'

'The knives came back.'

'And?'

'They're positive for Rachel and Jack's blood and DNA.'

Jaggerbombs always make me puke. I felt like I was after drinking five of them, said: 'That's impossible.'

'The science doesn't lie.'

'It does now. Why would I do it? It's only money. Not enough to do...what they're saying I did.'

'Temporary insanity is very powerful, triggered by multiple factors, and can literally cause moments of pure madness. In your case the cause didn't matter. You were unhinged from reality.'

'It's fuckin pure bananas. Tell them to run the test again.'

'It's a valid result.'

'Ah Christ, where do we go from here?'

'Treatment. Talking. Medication.'

'Tablets?'

'Anti-psychotic drugs. They should help with the persistent delusions.'

'I don't want to kill anyone. I never did.'

'I need you to start accepting where you are if you are to build up a proper sense of what's *real* and what's *imaginary*.'

'Do you really think it was me?'

'The science says so.'

'But what do *you* think?'

'My personal opinion doesn't matter.'

'It matters to me. Do you think I'm guilty?'

'Guilty? No. Responsible? Yes.'

'Has anyone even checked to see if there's another version of me in a coma in Athlone?'

'Yes.'

'And?'

'And I think I need to write you that prescription today.'

## Letter to Karen

Another month went. That song, David Bowie, *Five Years,* looping and looping and looping. A soundtrack to the scene. I thought of a calm afternoon with cool air on Connaught Street. We were in *Vinny's.* I was there with Jack, and Bowie was on the jukebox. We were drinking cans and killing the day. Sales made, money made, lushing it up. Lushing down the hours, pushing down the sun, snake charming the moon into drunk oblivion. Inhibiting the fear, letting the meaning take hold, letting the music swim.

And now I was in an asylum. Bunk beds. Bars. Radio static in the distance. Tinged yellow light. Steel bowl for the toilet. Concrete floor. I forgot what day it was. Most days were the same anyway. Breakfast. Exercise. Back to the ward.

I thought back on them evenings driving drunk from Portlaoise. Just driving in the dark, hoping a city of answers might appear over the next hill. Some wild Vegas of life discovery and meaning. Maybe that's where I really started to break. *Fragment* as Amanda called it. She said I should apologise to the people I've hurt so I wrote a letter to Karen. I knew it was pointless but it felt good to get everything out. Clear the air. Maybe give her some closure. Explain that the prostitute I rode in Madrid wasn't even fuckin real. You know? That kind of thing.

Ask me if she wrote back.

Did she write back?

Did she fuck write back. Bitch.

## Germany and everything

Damien arrived a week later and said my case had come up. And wasn't it great news? It would all be over soon. A date was set for next month. Said he was a bit nervous because he had never done a murder trial before. Really? I said. I would have never guessed. And has there been any developments I should know about?

He thought, said, oh yeah. The knives came back. Did anyone tell you?

Yes, Damien. Amanda mentioned it.

Oh, right. He said. They had Jack and Rachel's blood on them.

I doubt that, I told him. Cows maybe, sheep. Pigs.

No, he said. The DNA matched, it went to Germany and everything, and they're fairly sure. It's the proof they were looking for so they're going to go ahead now.

Can we get a second opinion?

He looked at the table, thought, and said I don't think so. But *I'll ask.*

Do, good man. *Ask.*

I have to go then, he said.

Where you off to?

The charity shop, he said. To pick up a new suit. For the trial.

We were all friends with this ride once and one day she told a story in the pub and everybody laughed. The following week I heard her boyfriend tell the same story and nobody gave a fuck. This is what I'm talking about. Most lads my age did ok for a while. We were able to hide the madness during the booms and then the recessions.

First there was money everywhere. So we could travel.

Buy houses. Drink. Eat. Buy cars. Buy women. Buy drugs. Didn't matter cos everyone was doing it. If you didn't like where you were, you could buy your way out. Go to the bank, get another loan, another credit card. Go to another country. Get married. Get divorced. Have a kid. Crash the car. Buy another. Go to rehab. Start again. Then the recessions came and that was ok too. Because everyone was broke. Give back the car. Downsize the house. Split from the woman. Drink more at home. Buy cheaper drugs. Let the credit cards bounce. Let the loans go by in a soft unpaid cloud.

Letters from debt collectors. Eviction notices. Calls from banks. Court injunctions. Repossession orders. Unpaid bill phones. Go back to prepaid. Change the number. Buy cheap cider. Everyone was doing it. It was ok. It was all madness, but everyone was *mad* so it was ok. It was all normal. But then there's a point when that stops. You don't see it coming. Them days go out like a light and it's time to catch the next bus out of Baluba world. But some lads miss it. And they keep going the way they're going. You see them in the bookies at fifty years of age, roaring at the telly. Or fighting over games of pool, or card games in the pub, or up in court for sending pictures of their knob to young wans. Or smoking at pub doors and not a tooth in their head. And some lads end up in jail. And everyone thinks: Jez, he's fucked altogether. And that's me. Looking at real time for a crime I couldn't even remember. And where do you go from here?

Amanda said: 'Going to a trial is not the end of the world. We've made a lot of progress and I'll submit my report on the day.'

'I don't remember anything about knives, never mind killing anyone.'

'You wouldn't.'

'Or ever usin them for anythin except work.'

'Again, you wouldn't. It just proves we've been on the right track and oddly makes your insanity case even stronger.'

'I'd say I'm cooked.'

'Mental illness is a genuine defence. And you're genuinely mentally ill. There are options here. Don't lose faith.'

## *The Trial*

The day came. They knocked on the door, all confident and full of purpose. I thought of the slaughterhouse and how the cows were coaxed up the dark corridor to be stunned before being shot. The cows never knew what was coming but I had a fair idea. They led me out in chains and handed me over to the guards. A man guard and a woman guard. Holding my arms tight. Taking no chances. They brought me into the back of a van. With thin benches either side. The chains were padlocked to a hook on the floor. There was me and two other lads. All going to trial. One lad was in for drugs. The other for killing his father. And me.

We got there around ten. The courthouse in Athlone. They brought us round the back to avoid the swarm of journalists.

Parked up. Got out. Fresh air. Urban sounds.

Walked through the cheap doors and into the courthouse. Bleach washed floor. Pricks in suits going around the place. Smell like a primary school. It was all like a dodgy soap. They brought us to a room. Smoky place with big windows. Fed us with breakfast rolls while we waited. Eggs, sausages, ketchup, the works. Damien was there. Newly creased suit. Blue eyed scorched pallor. I asked him what the prognosis for the day was. He told me not to worry. Suspended sentence probably. Might have to accept two years. Be out in nine months after psychological evaluation. I had a clean record. The judge had a lenient reputation. It was all sound. He was hoping it wouldn't take too long because he had another job delivering Chinese takeaways and he wanted to be home in time. I asked him what about Amanda and he said she wasn't allowed testify. I asked him why and he didn't know, just his boss at the office said she couldn't talk on my behalf, but don't worry, he had read the report and knew it off by heart.

Then there was a spare box of spicy wedges and he started eating them. He cut open the yellow sachets of mayonnaise and made a soft white mountain and used it as a dip.

And then we were called.

Through a large wooden door. There was a smell of mass and rich people's houses. It reminded me of being an altar boy when we were young. And you'd have to walk up the aisles and all the crowd would be looking at you. Except now they hated me. Even Rachel's family were there. Glaring. Playing the tabloid game. Tearful. Pockets full of speeches for after the sentence. Did they not know about Anthony? Did they really believe it was all *me*?

The judge arrived. Asked us to sit down. Lads in wigs were going around the place. There was evidence read out by the prosecution. I was a callous and cold brutal killer.

Known for strange behaviour and alcohol abuse.

An aloof sort of man that worked a lot and often made customers feel uncomfortable.

Killing Jack was an act of savagery comparable only to the crimes of Mexican cartels or Sicilian Godfathers.

And Rachel had been vulnerable. An unfortunate victim caught in the crossfire of a savage gangland feud. I had disposed of her with a complete disregard for human life and common decency. Possibly even enjoyed the sick brutality of it.

And both killings were done to cause the maximum amount of pain and send a terrifying message to the public – that criminals like me are untouchable.

Then it was Damien's turn. He did his best. Argued the case. But the judge wasn't impressed. Had to ask him to speak up a few times. I could hardly hear him myself. Something about a medical report, evaluation. And he was after getting mayonnaise on the collar of his jacket and it looked fucking cat altogether.

Then the judge asked the jury to go and think hard about justice.

They were back after ten minutes. People were still out

smoking. I thought I heard gratification in the woman's voice as she read the verdict.

Pure stone guilty.

Some people sighed, most people clapped. Rachel's family cried and hugged each other. Then the judge said a few things I didn't hear. Sure I was gone pure weak. Eventually the gravity came through. Two life sentences. Bang bang. Back to back. No parole for at least eighteen years. Case adjourned.

I looked at Damien and he was gone an unsure shade of speechless purple, like someone was after stealing all his clothes and he was afraid to ask for them back.

Then.

Woman guard. Man guard. Van and chains. They brought me out the front door this time. Part of the drama, the new age public stoning, media crucifixion. Outside, I took in my last breath of fresh air. Confused, scared. There was such a swarm of microphones and camera flashes that we were stalled for a good thirty seconds. In the middle of it all I looked up, sensed something, someone, looking at me intently. It was Karen. She was standing against a tree across the road. Arms folded, crying. I remembered seeing her again that night outside the Bank of Ireland on Church Street. Like she was there for me, just for me, a gift from the gods. All we'd been through and we hadn't even started. I wanted to wave but I couldn't with the handcuffs. Then I was pushed into the van again. On my own this time.

The drug dealer got off.

The man that killed his father was sent to Dundrum for psychological care.

I was in Portlaoise prison in time for the six o'clock news.

And I was the main story.

## *Real time*

I was lying on the bunk, looking at the concrete ceiling, thinking about all this. It was six months later. Portlaoise was a lonely place. The most secure prison in Europe. Full of IRA lads and cartel gangsters. The nature of my crime gave me some credibility and I was generally left alone. Eat the food, do the exercise, stay quiet. Damien was working on the appeal. Had assured me it was too harsh a sentence, unprecedented under the circumstances. And there was question marks over the evidence. I asked him what the question marks were and he wasn't sure. Just there was a case last week that collapsed due to bad forensics. He heard someone talking about it in the Chinese last night.

Amanda still came once a week. Made me feel less distanced from reality. Turns out I hadn't been listening to people for years. They'd been talking but I hadn't heard a word they'd said. I'd just be waiting for the tone, the vocal lilt or drop, and then answer with something half hearted. Now I could hear again. And see the colours of language and hear the song of how people really felt. It was a bit like my blood was getting warmer. And after a while, I started to forget about Marilyn. And Columba and Cathy and the whole lot. Being in jail helped. The concrete certainty and the routine. I stopped thinking about other realities and quantum jumps. I was sober too and on the medication. Soon enough, I was just me. The last layer of the fucked up onion. And I was ready to live again. Except I had to somehow do two life sentences first.

Messy.

## *Keyboard*

Next thing. Anthony got caught. He was coming down from the North with a boot full of drugs and guns and the PSNI pulled him over. It worked out great because they reported him to the guards in the South and they searched his house, which led them to a warehouse, where they found a few handy pieces of evidence.

Things like:

The actual knives used to kill Rachel and Jack.

Rachel's bloodstained clothes.

A computer with videos of the whole torture scene.

Traces of semen on the keyboard.

A bit more than circumstantial.

Amanda that told me. I said: 'How's that for indicators?'

'It certainly gets you off the cross.'

'So I'm not mad?'

'Oh, no. You're mentally ill. There's no doubt about that. Ironically, it took an incident like this to diagnose you.'

'It's a long incident. Why were they so sure it was me?'

'One of the guards on your case worked for Anthony. Owed him a few favours apparently.'

'So he planted the DNA on the knives?'

'We're waiting for word on that. But it's enough to register your conviction as unsafe. Everyone wanted an easy win with you. It was important for public confidence to see someone get jailed. It's probably why they stopped me coming to the trial.'

'Probably why they sent me Damien too.'

'Regardless, even if you didn't commit the murders you were exhibiting some very dangerous behaviours and you needed help. I'd call this a good save.'

'Is that what you're goin to write on your report?'

'I'm going to make a case to get you released and still treat you as an outpatient.'

'Is that necessary?'

'I expect it'll be mandatory - you *did* steal the money and abscond but we can take time served into account for that - provided you continue treatment.'

'So what now? Where will I go?

'Athlone?'

'Home? What if Karen is still there?'

'I looked into that.'

'And?'

'She suffered a lot of intimidation and abuse from Rachel's family. Once they found out where you lived they made it impossible for her.'

'So she's gone?'

'Yes. And moved on.'

'Another fella?'

'An accountant from Moate.'

'Sounds about fuckin right.'

'At least you'll have somewhere to go back to. You owned the apartment, didn't you?'

'Yeah. Both of us did.'

'Well, you still own it. Except now you live alone. You'll probably have to buy her out eventually. I doubt she ever wants to see the place again.'

'Or me.'

'Some things can't be helped. Be thankful for the positives.'

## *Jammy John joe gets the Out of Jail Free card*

I heard nothing for a while. Except the radio. They let me have one now because I wasn't considered dangerous anymore. Like, they could trust me with a radio, I wouldn't serial kill it or anything.

Heard a few bits about my case. There was a lot of public controversy about how my conviction came about. Few big knobs throwing shapes. The word *tampering* was thrown around. And then it all died down and one day the guards came to my cell asked me to leave. I was listening to *Lyric Fm*. Something in a Sonata K with B Minor.

Next thing I was packing up my stuff and led out the door.
No apology or nothing.
Just off you go now.

I got the bus back home. Got off on Connaught Street. It was quiet except for a couple of lads talking outside the off licence and one or two coming in and out of the charity shop. It was like coming back from a year travelling – nothing had changed and yet everything felt different. Like you're a local and a stranger at the same time. A tourist in your own life.

Cars cruised by. Got a couple of odd looks from pedestrians, like I was a circus act and they weren't sure whether or not to stand and watch. I walked into the apartment complex and used my old key to get in the security gate. It still worked and I walked on by the letterboxes to the left. Out of pure compulsion, I checked to see was there any post. There was mostly junk and a few old battered bills with my name on them. Surprised Karen hadn't thrown them in the skip.

At the apartment. There was some graffiti on the door and the kitchen window was smashed but inside it was ok.

Cold, but ok.

The corridor was a bit stale and there was a hush when I

entered, like all the ghosts had to scamper because a human had come home. I tried the light and it came on. Not cut off. Good start. I walked to the bedroom and looked around and contemplated the quiet.

The sheets were a bit damp and the floors looked a bit mouldy but otherwise it seemed sound. My clothes were still in the wardrobe but they were no good and I'd have to throw them out. All Karen's stuff was gone except for a bottle of shampoo that she'd left in the bathroom. I smelled it and it still smelled of her. Her and the green shoes and the silver necklace and that taste like crushed orange and safety.

I put the bottle back and went to the kitchen. Same scene.

Sour milk in the fridge. Old dark dishes in the sink. The television had been pulled from the wall and there was a sample of scared wires and dusty boxes from old cable tv connections.

I sat on the couch and looked around and let the form settle.

What the fuck now?

## Rock 'n' Roll Suicide

The papers ran one last story and then left me alone. They were more interested in Anthony now. And the corruption thing. All the honest cops on the case had to wear masks in case Anthony's gang recognised them and tortured their families. And the court had to be done behind closed doors where you couldn't see the faces of the jury. Eventually he got the two life sentences aswell and the whole thing was finally over. Except I was stone broke. Needed money. Didn't fancy another sales job and the debt collecting crew would probably tell me to fuck off.

I needed something to keep the head right too.

Amanda said to be careful with triggers and stress.

And whatever I do, don't drink. It didn't suit me with the tablets.

That was tough. Sure all I knew was how to drink. Talk shite and buy pints. I was brilliant at it. I knew when to start and when to stop and how to keep going in between. And now I couldn't do it at all.

So instead I got a job in a pub.

It was *Vinny's*. The place across the road. Long shiny bar with good music and lots of regulars. I saw the sign that they were hiring and I walked in.

There was a cute blonde girl behind the counter. She introduced herself as Sandra. Said she was leaving the job to go back to college. And I'd be taking her hours. And would I mind that? Sounded alright. She was the owner's daughter so she could offer me the job right there.

I'll take it. I started Saturday night. Pulling pints and firing out cans. And odd one looking for whisky.

I'd heard about this. People that were off the drink getting jobs in pubs. And it somehow helps. You can see people getting drunk and talking shite. Can see yourself from the outside. And at the same time you're surrounded by it, so you don't feel like you're missing anything. You're getting the buzz but you're not drinking.

You'd see a fella come in sober. Decent lad. Five pints later he's a mess. Groping women. Pissing himself. Unsure what the problem is. Then a woman comes in and orders a tap water with ice and lemon. Hangs there for a while until some fella offers her a drink.

What's that, honey?

That's a gin and tonic, baby.

Fill it up there, John joe. Let's get the session going.

And there's your man that hasn't drank for twenty years but still comes in and has a coffee and does the crossword. And the two lads from the buildings. Transit van. Three pints every evening and home. And here's lonely Martin drinking to pass the time. He'll bring in the kegs and pick you up the lemons in the shop when you run out. He'll even get a bag of ice and do the lotto for the customers on the way back. All for a pint on the house.

And on the story goes. Everyone's got a history. Everyone's got a tale, a tragedy and a tear. Everyone's half way down the endless glass.

I told all this to Amanda.

She listened and said: 'You're glorifying alcohol.'

'You didn't hear the tragedy part.'

We were in Clonbrusk Medical centre. Pine desks. Chairs that you might find in a bank. She was looking good. Still husky, but different. Black lace top and her hair down. Big into blue eye contact.

She continued: 'I know you said it helps to be close to drink, but it's still asking for trouble.'

'I'm in the flat on my own. No woman. No job. I need an outlet.'

'Is there nothing else you could do?'

'Nothing else I'm really good at. Up until now it's been all *sales* and *slaughterhouses*. None of them worked out too good.'

'And how's the mind? Anything you're worried about?

Anything unusual?'

'Would I know?'

'Any thoughts of alternative realities? Anything like that?'

I thought, said: 'No. And I haven't thought about anythin like that for weeks.'

'Sleeping ok?'

'The medication helps.'

'This is real progress.'

'I'm surprised myself.'

'I don't want to get too excited – but either way, I think we can start cutting down our sessions.'

'By how much?'

'Let's give it a month before we see each other again.'

'Really?'

'Yes, and if there's no deterioration I'll be able to certify you as recovered.'

'From what exactly?'

'Schizoid related nervous breakdown.'

'Is that what it's called?'

'It's as close as we'll get. The crucial thing is your indicators are negative, the medication is effective, and you feel ok.'

'True.'

She looked at the notes again, said: 'Oh, yes. I wanted to ask you something.'

'What was that?'

'Knowing when people are going to die.'

'Remind me again.'

'You'd see somebody and think: They'll be dead in five years from…a piano falling on their head or something…'

'Oh, that. Yeah. Columba called it second sight. Proof that I'm not crazy.'

'Columba was imaginary, remember?'

'I know.'

'Anything like that lately? Any morbid premonitions?'

'Not really.'

'Not *really*?'
'Very little.'
'See these are the things we need to stamp out.'
'That's always been there. For years. I don't think it's connected.'
'Has it happened recently?'
'Once.'
'With who?'
'It doesn't matter.'
'It does, actually. It matters a lot. You need to get this out.'
'I don't want to go there.'
'You are *here* because you have to go *there*. Now tell me.'
'It was nothin major.'
'Ok, let's hear it.'
Beat.
'It was about *you*.'

She looked a bit concerned, pale under the tan, said: 'Who? Me?'

'Yeah.'

Her mouth quivered slightly, and she said: 'I don't think that's something you need to worry about.'

'See, I didn't want to tell you.'
'It's a delusion. But tell me anyway.'
'You get strangled by a patient.'
'Wh....when?'
'Before our next appointment.'

She thought, said: 'Well ok. This is perfect in a way. Because when I come back you'll know it's imaginary and it will eradicate that final delusion.'

'Ok. And if you don't?'

She smiled, said: 'Then I guess Columba was right all along....'

## *Russia's greatest love machine*

Work that night was busy. Some party on. Someone was fifty. They drank pints, whisky, wine. The till rang with cash and coins. The music was loud. They had a band in singing Credence Clearwater Revival and Dire Straits and Roy Orbison and all the classics.

*Sultans of Swing.*

The crowd got bigger, difficult to manage. Sandra had to step in and help me. She was better at the bar than me. A lifetime of experience. In the blood. She could hold ten orders in her head, count change, fire out bags of Tayto. We got on well. Good rhythm. Took half the bar each and kept the punters happy.

It went on late, through closing time. We eventually got the last of them out at two in the morning. Cleaned the place up and she pulled a pint for herself.

Offered me one. I said: 'I don't drink.'

She had a nice posh voice that cracked a bit at the end. Sophisticated and common. One of your own wherever she was. Socially multi-lingual. Awful fuckin attractive.

She said: 'You don't drink?'

'No.'

'I'm sure I saw you in here before having a pint?'

'Yeah. I gave up.'

'Is that part of your parole?'

'I'm not on parole. I was cleared.'

'Oh, so it's an AA thing?'

'Not exactly.'

'Have a coke then?'

'I'll have a Cidona, thanks.'

'Cidona it is.'

She got them. We took seats at the counter. She was wearing a short denim skirt, strong legs, like a dancer. Low cut top and her hair was loose, just below her shoulders.

We talked. She was studying something to do with earthquakes. Soft skin, no epidermal loss. Some kind of subtle glitter around her eyes. Delicate fingers. I drank the Cidona.

She said: 'I have a confession to make.'

'Go for it.'

'I'm obsessed with serial killers.'

'What's that go to do with me?'

'Nothin *now*. But when I read your story. And then you came in for a job...'

'You hired me because...'

'I was...am extremely attracted to you.'

'Sorry to burst your bubble.'

'That's the thing. It didn't burst.'

'I'm no Jack the Ripper....'

'It doesn't matter anymore. What happened to the girl you were with?'

'Karen? She's gone.'

'I used to see you together around town. You never looked happy.'

'It was a difficult time.'

The jukebox was on random with *REM, Everybody Hurts*. A melting sadness, a massage of tough memories. She said: 'So it's over?'

'Long gone.'

'I knew her brother.'

'Him.'

'Him. Is he a priest now?'

'No, last I heard he was getting married.'

'Funny.'

'Her whole family are all clowns really. What about you?'

'Do I have a man?'

'Yeah.'

'No. I'm too fucked up.'

'You don't look fucked up.'

'You don't know me.'

'I know *fucked up*.'

'I think that's why I like you.'
'We could cancel each other out and be normal.'
'Or be super crazy.'
'I'm just back from super crazy. Thanks anyway.'
'Are you sure you don't want a real drink?'
'I'm sure I want one. I know I shouldn't.'
'What harm can it do?'
'I'm just out of Portlaoise after being accused of double murder.'
'But you didn't do it. Have a whisky. I want to see the real you.'
'This is the real me.'
'No it's not. I've seen drinkers my whole life. Some people are only themselves when drunk. The rest of the time they're pretending through the sober fog.'
'Still. I won't chance it.'
'I think you will. I think you already have.'

She put her hand between my legs, massaged softly. I was hard in seconds. It had been nearly a year.

'What was your favourite drink? Look around. We're in this bar. Just the two of us. All night if we want. We don't even have to pay. It's unlimited time, baby.'

I gave it a second. Pretended to resist, just for the record. Then went: 'I've been craving a vodka.'

She massaged harder. 'Vodka and....?'

'Diet coke.'

She went to get them. I was shaking. Double abstinence about to break. Drink and riding. I was coming alive by the second. The mad bitch was right. I had been a dead man walking. Until now. Fuck the tablets, Amanda, the whole lot. Time to live.

She came back. Left the glass on the counter. I could tell it was a double. Diet coke beside it. 'Fill your own mixer.' She said, then went on her knees and wrapped her mouth around me.

We both swallowed. Me the vodka. Her my glory. We both confessed to liking the taste and wanting more.

So we took a few bottles from the top shelf and went

upstairs.

It was well kept. Wood floor. Bedroom to the left. We went in there, let the wonder fly through the serene dawn. Her sheets were light. Silk pillows. She came like a tigress. We slept naked. Warm and astounded, intoxicated and free.

## *Don't let them cure you*

There goes the month, like a blood red summer. Tried to keep the drinking calm but hadn't a hope with Sandra. When we weren't working we were drinking or sleeping together. It was all sweat and fireworks and intimacy under moonlight. We spent most of the time in her apartment over the pub. Her father was gone for three months to the South of France so she ran the place. Had it all to herself. It was perfect.

Then the appointment with Amanda came around. I stayed in my own place the night before because I wanted to be sober and fresh. I wasn't going to tell her about the drinking. Just wanted to finish up with her and start living.

Today was the day. I was feeling stiff and tired, must have slept bad. So much for feeling fresh. I got into the car and the diesel light came on. That was unusual. It was usually good on juice and I had put twenty euro in the tank yesterday. Made a mental note to check for a leak.

I still had some time so I called over to Sandra. The bedroom was spacious, red carpet. She had music on. Guns n' Roses *So fine*.

She was in a black silk shirt and naked besides. Her figure was a causal model, catwalk indifferent. Her sun coloured hair was thin and light on her shoulders. She was drinking a Jack Daniels and coke through a straw. Standing at the end of the bed, she asked: 'What time is your appointment?'

'2pm.'

'Why do you still need to go there?'

'Part of my release.'

'Do they still think you're a psycho?'

'Few other things to iron out. Today should be one of the last appointments.'

'Are you feeling cured?'

'Since I met you?'

'Yes.'
'It's only been a month.'
'It has.'
'I like the feeling of you inside me. It's different.'
'How so?'
'More personal. I can feel…all of you.'
'I'm there. All of me.'
She shrugged, said: 'Am I enough for you?'
'What do you mean?'
'I want to be everything. I want us to be complete. I don't want anything left out.'
'It's pure. It's real. It's…unlike anything I've ever had.'
'I missed you last night.'
'Me too.'
'Where did you go?'
'I was there. At home.'
'Really?'
'Yeah, why?'
'I got lonely and called by and the lights were off. And your phone was dead.'
'Maybe I was asleep.'
'And your car was gone.'
'I don't think so. Are you sure?'
'Positive. It doesn't matter. Just, I was worried.'
'Don't worry. I have to go.'

Got to the car. Turned the ignition. There was a pain in my right hand, like I was after spending the day before loading bales into a trailer. *Siegel im Seigel* came through from *Lyric FM*. Had a soothing air about it. Let it run, brought me down Pearse Street and over the bridge. Down by the Radisson and through the lights. Took a left at Beechpark. Through the roundabout and a right for the medical centre.

Parked up. Let the song finish. Let the sun suffer through the window. Felt the warm rays on my chest. The news came through. Job losses, political scandals, a murder in Dublin.

Got out. Walked over. Went through the automatic doors.

It was quiet. White walls. A smell like strong lemon. My room with Amanda was upstairs. I went up. Down a corridor. Found it. R503. Thick wood door. I knocked. She usually shouted to come in. Today she didn't. I checked my watch. I wasn't early.

Knocked again. Nothing. Went to the reception. There was a woman there with glasses. I asked about Amanda. She frowned, looked at her watch, said: 'She should be here.' Then asked: 'Is she not up there?'

'No.'

'Did you knock?'

'I did.'

'And what happened?'

'Nobody answered.'

'Really? That's odd.'

'Tis.'

'Are you sure you have the right day and time?'

'I do.'

'Ok. Let me take your number and I'll look into it and get back to you.'

'She usually comes down from Dublin so maybe there's a delay?'

'Yeah. Hmm. Possible. Let me call you if I hear anything.'

'Do.'

I was walking away when she said: 'Oh, hang on. The room's been changed. I can see it here.'

'Oh, so she's *here*?'

She squinted at the computer again. 'I...think so. There seeems to be a double booking. Are you sure you have the right day?'

'I am.'

'Ok, and you're John joe?'

'That's right.'

'There's a note here on your account.'

'What does it say?'

'Ok, go on up to Room 506. Let me know if there's anyone there. Sometimes they rotate the counsellors so you may have someone temporary for today.'

'Temporary?'

'Yes. If a therapist is sick or can't come. Maybe just check it out first and come back to me.'

Walked up the stairs again. Through the anxious sun and a racing mind. Searched the numbers until I found room 506. I knocked and a familiar voice answered with: 'Come in.'

So I pushed down the handle and walked inside.